Hobcaw Point

TAYLOR RICKARD

AUSXIP PUBLISHING

Print ISBN: 9780645108484

Edited by Rosa Alonso
Cover Design by Mary Draganis
Hobcaw Point Map courtesy of the U.S. Geological Survey
Interior design by AUSXIP Publishing

Printed in the United States

AUSXIP Publishing
Level 13 Suite 1A,
465 Victoria Avenue,
Chatswood NSW 2067
Australia
www.ausxippublishing.com

DEDICATION

This story is the product of my memories of my beloved grandmother, Vermelle Holeman Galbreath, and my great grand aunt, Ervinia Smith Bishop, two amazing women who loved history – and me! They were both genealogists who hauled me around the South every summer to visit museums, battlefields, cemeteries, and family landmarks until Southern history and culture were engrained in my heart and mind. The love they had for Charleston and its wonderful history and culture is part of this story and my tribute to them. It is also dedicated to my friend and colleague, Nene Adams, who, like me, grew up in the South and wrote her stories from her heart. Twenty years ago, she told me I needed to write this story. Nene, wherever your soul is now – here it is, finally. I still miss you.

ACKNOWLEDGMENTS

I would like to thank Dr. Shireen Soomro for her persistent encouragement to get this story written.

Rosa Alonso for her patience in getting this story readable.

As always, my partner Morgan Sams for his amazing patience and support when I get focused on writing.

Hobcaw Point Map

LONG POINT RD

Hobcaw
Point

Hobcaw Creek

10

Roughly the
original channel
and harbor...

Cemetery

MOLASSES LN

COINBOW DR

BAMPFIELD DR

HOBCAW DR

E HOBCAW DR

**Hobcaw
Point**

o River

Molasses Creek

CHAPTER 1

AMANDA SHERMAN DROVE HER BEAT UP JEEP Wrangler down Molasses Lane to the even more bumpy ride down Hobcaw Drive to the unnamed road paved with crushed oyster shells that led to the site of the old shipyard on Hobcaw Creek. The good people of Charleston County, South Carolina, specifically the rapidly growing town of Mount Pleasant, wanted a fancy marina or yacht club to bolster their attractiveness to the upper middle class that were moving into the area.

On the other hand, the county didn't have a whole lot of money. Amanda smiled to herself, considering the irony of the situation. They'd hired her because she was young for a civil engineer, and had only done one other project on her own. So, she was cheap. But the county wanted something that didn't look cheap. In fact, her instructions were to build them something that looked like it had its roots in South Carolina history. And they had sent her off to do a site survey down on this undeveloped hunk of land, which evidently had once been a shipyard, but that was long ago. Her own forefather had razed the place at the end of the Civil War.

She parked her Jeep, opened the rear gate, and pulled out a plat map and several aerial photographs. She had studied them intensely before she had come out to the site, but wanted to refresh her memory one more time before she picked up her camera and her small voice recorder and started her site survey.

She looked around, trying to decide where to start. Set several hundred yards back from the natural harbor was a huge old live oak tree, spreading its branches over what was left of a wrought iron fence around what was obviously an old family cemetery. Amanda shook her head. Having a cemetery on the grounds made things more complicated – as if they weren't already. The county wanted to take the property by eminent domain, but to do so meant they had to find the owners. Ah, well, now they had to find the family anyway to get permission to move the graves. She started taking photographs, commenting on each one in her voice recorder as she went.

THE OLD MAN, dressed in a loose shirt, britches and boots, sat on top of one of the grave stones. He was grumping about the woman who was invading his domain without an invitation. "What doth she desire with my land?"

A small woman dressed in a loose gingham dress laid a

gentle hand on his shoulder. "Husband, let it rest. Remember that is it no longer our land, but is that of our dear granddaughter. She will have to know and come to defend what is our family's."

The old man grumped some more. "As if she even knew what she has. I do na think a single member of the family has seen our deed in generations. For if they did, they would know what they had here."

"She will save our land, Samuel. There is nary a Balle who could willingly let this land be taken. Caitlin is no different."

The old man harumphed, then let out a low-pitched whistle.

Two small, brown creatures popped up out of the long grass surrounding the cemetery. "You called, Laird?" they voiced together.

"Yes, yes, I did. See that woman walking around the property? Go see if you can find out what she is doing."

The two little creatures disappeared into the tall grass without saying a word.

"Now we wait."

CAITLIN BALLE STOMPED up on her front porch, juggling an armful of papers as she tried to unlock her front door. After she dropped half of the folders in her arms on the porch, she managed to unlock the door. She reached in and dropped the remaining files on the small table in the hall, then bent down to collect her files. Adding them to the pile already on the table, she bent again to gather up the mail that had been shoved through the slot in her door.

She flipped through the collection of ads and bills and stopped cold at the green card with the postal service insignia. It was a notice of an attempt to deliver a certified letter that required a signature. Caitlin shook her head. She wondered who the hell was sending her certified mail. Today was Wednesday; maybe she could get to the post office on Saturday to pick up the letter. It would just have to wait until then.

She picked up her folders and the little pile of mail and wandered into her office, grumbling as she went. She dropped the pile of folders in the middle of her desk, then flipped through the mail again, discarding the advertisements in the trash, setting the bills in a small pile, and scanning the rest of the mail. In addition to the notification about the certified letter from someone, there was an invitation from the Charleston Historical Society to an event on Saturday night. There was also a note from her mother, threatening her with vile retribution if she did not attend the event.

She sat back in her desk chair and looked around the room. This house pre-dated the Revolutionary War, having been built as her great, great, however many greats grandfather's town house in Charleston around 1763. Over the years, the family had maintained and modernized it, but had kept the colonial flavor and, in many cases, the original architecture. This room had been Samuel Balle's office. It was lined with bookshelves on three walls, with windows out onto the side yard on the fourth. A still-working fireplace was in the center of the wall facing the windows with two portraits over the mantle.

"Grandma Siobhan, why can't my mother stop treating me like a ten-year-old?" she asked the portrait of the blue-eyed brunette smiling gently down on her from the portrait. She shook her head and sighed.

It took a few minutes to put the files from the Charleston Museum back in order. The board of directors wanted a new exhibit on colonial life in the South Carolina Lowcountry, but didn't want to spend a whole lot of money on adding new items to the collection. She would have to work with what they had stashed in the archives. The pile of folders included the descriptions and photos of all the items in storage.

Caitlin shook her head. Getting a job with the oldest museum in the country was a plum for the recently awarded Doctor of History. Rather than going on to a post-doc position, she took the route to being a museum curator. The Charleston Museum, the oldest museum in America, was still a small, community and regionally oriented museum. It was an ideal starting point for an ambitious young curator. Fortunately, her family connections in old Charleston society got her the introductions she needed, but it was her sterling academic record that actually got her the position.

She sighed and settled in to evaluate the materials she had available to put together a new exhibit from the existing collection. She had to report to the board of directors in less than two weeks.

AMANDA WALKED into the county board meeting on Thursday afternoon with a roll of drawings under one arm and a flash drive with pictures in her pocket. She turned on the laptop at the podium in the room to boot up and posted the drawings on the wall on both sides of the central screen.

The board members started to file into the room, chatting and collecting bottles of water or cups of coffee from the table at the side of the room. Amanda shook her shoulders, trying to relax before she began her presentation.

Finally, the chairman of the board, Mr. Pinkney, came in and gaveled the congregated attendants to order. "All right, Ms. Sherman, tell us what you've found."

Amanda cleared her throat and sent the first image from her thumb drive to the screen at the front of the room. "Ladies and gentlemen, as you can see from the aerial photograph, we have a site that, on first appearances, presents an ideal location for a natural harbor and a multi-purpose recreational site. But look closer..."

Amanda went on, illustrating the challenges that the site presented. The harbor was heavily silted, and there were old stumps from the original piers still buried in the mud. There were remaining foundations from various antebellum buildings located around the property. Finally, there was the issue of the cemetery. "I know that there is still family remaining in the area, as demonstrated by the eminent domain action being taken. Under South Carolina law, to move a cemetery requires the consent of the living family. So, in addition to pursuing a successful eminent domain action, we will have to acquire separate consent to move the cemetery to a location of the family's choosing. In summary, we have a potential historical site, a family cemetery, and a probably expensive dredging operation needed to clear the harbor. These are some real challenges that we will have to face and resolve to proceed with this project."

Pinkney looked around the room. "We will have to take your findings under consideration, Ms. Sherman. Shall we reconvene next Thursday at the same time to review our decision? In the meantime, Ms. Sherman, would you expand your site evaluation to determine any alternatives available? And there is an event at the Historical Society tomorrow night. Can I invite you to attend? I somehow suspect we will have to persuade the membership to our, um, point of view on the resolution of the situation out at Hobcaw Point, and your presence may be of some political use."

"Certainly, Mr. Pinkney. When and where, sir?"

"Well, my wife and I are attending, so shall we pick you up at, say, seven?"

"Certainly. Um, what is the dress code for this event?"

"Oh, it's one of their usual cocktail parties."

"I'll be ready, sir."

LATER THAT EVENING, two small brown creatures sat at the foot of the enormous old oak tree, waiting for the Laird to show up. He was not going to be happy with what they had to report.

After waiting a few minutes, the old man showed up and took up his position on top of the gravestone. "So, what news, Grear?" he asked abruptly.

The male figure cleared his throat and looked up into the tree above him, where he saw the young woman, Ciara, sitting on a branch, glaring down at him.

He cleared his throat again and began his report. "Well, sir, I be thinking they are planning some sort of harbor site for modern boats, but the old buildings and pilings and such are going to be a problem. And they said they needed to do something to the harbor, but I dinna understand what it was."

The old man scratched at his beard. "Put it back the way it was as a working harbor?"

"Nae, sir. Something new and modern, not to build ships but to keep boats for families to go out and play."

"Boats for play? What insanity be this? Boats are nae for play!! And this is a shipyard, not a place for silly rowboats."

Kade spoke up, her voice squeaky and shrill, even though she was whispering. "'Tis nae the worst of it, sir. They want to move the cemetery."

Above them, Ciara shrieked, a bone-rattling, glass-breaking cry of despair if ever there was one.

"So, they want to finish what that cretin Sherman did during the War of Northern Aggression, do they? Well, we shall see about that. We shall see."

SEVEN O'CLOCK FRIDAY night rolled around and Amanda stood in the middle of her apartment living room, basically twitching. She was dressed in a simple black cocktail dress, with silver jewelry and black pumps with two-inch heels. Her hair, somewhere between honey blonde and light brown, was bound back in a French twist. All in all, she looked very sophisticated with her little black dress and grown-up hair style. She felt like a kid playing dress up. She was far more comfortable in her khaki shorts, hiking boots, and polo shirts.

She could hear her mother's laughing voice in her head. "Yes, honey, you do look good in drag. I know, I know, you hate it, but you really are a lovely woman."

She took a deep breath, picked up her shawl and purse, and headed out to meet the Pinkneys downstairs.

Mr. Pinkney pulled into the apartment building's driveway just as she stepped outside, driving his overgrown silver Cadillac. His fifty-something year old wife was sitting in the passenger seat, wearing a soft pink cocktail dress with a decolletage a little too low for her age. Once she had been Miss South Carolina, and somehow, she had never gotten past the image she thought went with that title.

Amanda settled in the back seat and immediately was subjected to a lecture from Pinkney. He listed all the people on the board of the Historical Society that she would need to butter up during this and future social events. If the Historical Society decided to hold on to Hobcaw Point as a potential archeological site, the hopes for building a proper marina would go down the drain.

The names and their respective positions went in one ear and out the other. Amanda was not good at remembering names unless she had a face to go with them. She was worse at playing social politics.

At the back of her mind was a visual image of her

opportunity for building a beautiful marina flushing down the toilet.

CAITLIN FOUND her mother standing in the entrance to the Historical Society building on Meeting Street, clearly waiting for her. "Good evening, Mother."

Harriet Balle looked at her daughter with a very critical eye. "Well, it took you long enough to get here, daughter. And did you have to dress so... so... blandly?"

"Mother, I am here as a historian, not as a woman on the hunt for a man. This is a working evening for me – and not as a potential courtesan."

Harriet's' face turned an unpleasant shade of puce. Though the woman did not raise her voice – in fact, she lowered it so as not to be heard by those around her – the diatribe that came from her lips was one that Caitlin had heard many times. "I am doing this for your good, daughter. You need a man to take care of you. You need to get married to carry on the line. Why do you think I signed you up for the St. Cecelia's Cotillion? So you could meet the right kind of man. Why do you think I come to these events and drag you with me? So you could meet the right kind of man. Why do you think I was so upset when you went to school in North Carolina and was so grateful that you didn't drag back some low-class tar heel? And why did you have to go off to graduate school in the first place? You didn't have to be some bluestocking. You could have worked with the Historical Society or the Huguenot Society and stayed here. But no—"

She was interrupted by the arrival of Caitlin's boss, the curator of Historical Archaeology, Dr. Sarah Highsmith. "Oh, good, Dr. Balle, I'm glad you're here."

"Dr. Highsmith, I'd like to introduce my mother, Mrs. Stephen Balle."

"Mrs. Balle, a pleasure to meet you. We are so happy to have your daughter on our staff." She turned to Caitlin. "There are a number of people I'd like you to meet. Shall we go?"

"Yes, please." Caitlin felt like Dr. Highsmith had thrown her a lifesaver. "Mother, I'll see you later."

Mrs. Balle stood there, looking rather frustrated.

The two scholars strolled into the main reception room and made a casual bee line to the bar, where they both acquired glasses of mediocre white wine.

Dr. Highsmith looked amused. "You looked like you needed rescuing."

"I did. My mother's values and expectations never made it out of the 1950s, which is a bit of a conundrum, since she wasn't born until 1967. You would think the decade of change would have given her a more, um, progressive view of the world. It didn't. God, my grandmother is more liberal than she is."

"Well, I do understand. It took my mother almost twenty years to realize that I was simply never going to marry a man. She sure threw enough of them in my path before she gave up."

"Oh, lord. You should see her latest idea. She suggested I chase after Emerson Carteret, who is single – again. That drunkard is fifteen years older than me, has just gone through his third divorce, and has a clear preference for young, busty blonds, which I definitely am NOT."

"Well, put aside your thoughts of competing with busty blondes for the biggest lush in Charleston and let's go chat up your ideas for a colonial lifestyles exhibit. I particularly like your idea of juxtaposing the three different classes – builders, merchants and craftsmen, and slaves, so we can see them side by side."

"You know, I went to my own family's traditions. The founder of my family was a ship builder who worked with various craftsmen and merchants. He had a house here in town – in fact, I live in it – as well as a home out by the shipyard. And he had a few slaves, but that was interesting, as he had skilled slaves. They had very different lives from the plantation hands."

"And I suspect we have plenty of stuff in the archives to demonstrate your ideas very clearly. So let's go sell the idea to the local history snobs."

The two women laughed at their own cynicism and strolled off to mix and sell the concepts for the new exhibit.

PINKNEY POKED Amanda in the side and pointed at the two women speaking with the chairman of the Historical Society. "That's Sarah Highsmith. She's the archaeologist at the museum, and if we are going to be able to get past the ruins out at Hobcaw, we are going to need her support."

The two of them worked their way toward the group Pinkney had pointed out, trying not to look too obvious. Tonight was just for introductions.

"Good evening, Dr. Highsmith." Pinkney was being smarmy.

"Good evening, Mr., uh, Pinkney." Sarah was cool, to say the least.

"It is so nice to see you here this evening, ma'am. May I introduce our new civil engineer, Ms. Amanda Sherman?"

"Ms. Sherman, good evening." The two women shook hands. "May I introduce Dr. Caitlin Balle, our newest curator?"

Pinkney smiled at Sarah. "I have known Caitlin for many years."

Pinkney took Highsmith's arm. "May I have a word with you?" They stepped aside.

Amanda looked seriously uncomfortable.

Caitlin smiled slightly. "So, Ms. Sherman, have you been in Charleston long?"

"Not too long. About a month now. You have a beautiful city here."

"I hope you haven't gotten too much, um, reaction to your surname. There are plenty of old-school Charlestonians who still hold a grudge against William Tecumseh Sherman."

Amanda grimaced. "I fear my great-great grandfather did not endear himself to many Southerners. I try to go by Amanda as quickly as I can."

Caitlin laughed softly. "Well, then, you must call me Caitlin and I will call you Amanda."

Just then, Pinkney and Highsmith rejoined them, with Highsmith looking more than slightly annoyed. They bid one another good evening and continued making their rounds at the reception.

CAITLIN HAULED herself out of bed, groaning because sleeping in on a Saturday was one of her personal indulgences, especially after an evening like the one before at the Historical Society's reception. She fixed a quick breakfast of coffee and cold cereal, dressed, and prepared to collect the certified letter that had been waiting for her since Wednesday.

"What the hell is this now? I thought I'd dealt with everything from Daddy's estate already," she groused out loud as she drove over to the post office. Madam Grumpy parked her car and went to stand in line at the one open window. There were three people in front of her and each had some sort of complicated problem to be resolved. Finally, she got to the window and presented the green card her postman had left for her. The clerk disappeared into the back of the office and didn't emerge for what felt like a half hour but was actually only ten minutes, carrying a thick envelope addressed to her father.

Silently, she took the envelope, nodded at the clerk, and left. She stared at the envelope with its return address of the Circuit Court. "All right. What the hell is this?" She thought for a minute and decided to go home, where she could look at the thick document in the comfort of her den with a fresh cup of coffee in hand.

"What the HELL!!!!" She threw the pile of papers on her desk. "We have owned that property for over three hundred and fifty years. We have paid the taxes every damned year. Yet they say we have no deed to the property and are trying to claim it as abandoned. ABANDONED!

How do they think the family cemetery there makes it abandoned?!"

She picked up the phone on her desk and called her mother. "Where did Father keep the property deeds?"

"Good morning, Caitlin. How are you this morning? I'm fine, thank you for asking." Harriet's' voice dripped sarcasm, a not uncommon tone for dealing with her daughter.

"Good morning, Mother. That slime ball Henry Pinkney is trying to take Hobcaw from us. I need the deed."

"You have it somewhere in that antique you live in. He kept all of his papers there, as you well know."

Caitlin sighed. "Thank you, Mother. I'll look here."

"I don't know why you worry about that worthless piece of land, anyway. It's nothing but mud and marsh grass and ruined old foundations."

Caitlin sighed again. "And the family cemetery."

"Not since before the war, dear. Those moldy old bones don't mean a thing anymore." Before Caitlin could get a word in edgewise, Harriet went on. "By the way, did you get a chance to chat with Emerson last night? I ran into him briefly, but he was in the middle of a conversation with some other guests."

'Other guests,' Caitlin thought. 'Could it have been that wanna be Miss South Carolina?' She chose to ignore her mother's digging. "Good morning, Mother. I'll let you know what is going on."

She picked up her address book, looked up a name, and dialed the phone number.

"Elizabeth Dauntry."

"Hi, Beth. Caitlin here."

"Caitlin! How are you, girl? It's been way too long." Her college dorm mate had gotten a job with the local paper after they graduated, and they had drifted apart when Caitlin went to graduate school, seeing one another occasionally over the holidays.

"I'm doing well, overall. I got a job as a curator at the Charleston Museum, but I've got a problem and I hope you can help."

"You know I will help you, but I'm not sure what a junior reporter can do."

"Well, this should be right up your alley. What is Henry Pinkney trying to push through the county board?"

"Well, the latest hair up his ass is a plan to build a yacht club with various facilities – meeting rooms, restaurant, pool, to attract more upper middle-class residents over to Mt. Pleasant."

"Oh, okay. I understand. He's trying to take Hobcaw Point from me."

"Makes sense. If he can get it by eminent domain, he won't have to pay you or anyone else for the land for his little project."

"Yeah, well, we will see about that. If I think of anything you can do, I'll let you know."

"Until then, how about lunch, girlfriend? We need to catch up."

"In addition to saving a property that's been in my family forever, I've also got a new exhibit to mount, so things are a little busy, but maybe next week."

"Sounds good. Call me when you get free."

〜

THE GRAY BEARDED MAN, leaning in the corner of the library he had so lovingly built so many years before, scratched his cheek. "'That deed is here, right where I put it. Wish I could tell her where it is.'"

He returned to his usual haunt, sitting atop the tomb stone, to think.

CAITLIN SPENT all of Sunday digging through her father's files. She opened and went through every single file folder in both of the four drawer cabinets in the room. She filled multiple black garbage bags, consigning to the trash old utility and phone receipts from twenty years ago, ancient AAA membership cards that wouldn't bring a tow truck since she was in elementary school, and paid medical bills for relations who had long since joined the family members resting in one of several cemeteries in the area.

She found the deed to the house she was living in at 75 King Street, originally dated 1763. It was carefully encased in a museum quality archival crystal clear sleeve, as were the original architect's drawings for the brick house. She also found the deed to her mother's condominium over on Sullivan's Island, where her parents had retreated when her father retired. He had known he was dying and wanted to be near the ocean. But there was no deed to Hobcaw Point.

By about eight that evening, Caitlin was tired, dusty, hungry, and massively frustrated. She had found tax records reaching back to the 1870s, but no deed. She looked around the room at the twelve-foot-high shelves that covered three of the four walls, wrapping around the fire place and the door out to the hall, all filed with books, ledgers, and document boxes of various sorts and from various ages. Going through them all was a daunting task, one she suspected she would have to do in the coming days.

But for now, she needed food. Tomorrow she would figure out a way to slow Pinkney down.

She washed the smears of dust from her face and hands and beat the worst of the grime from her clothes, then walked two blocks north to Poogan's, a neighborhood Southern style restaurant that was a step up from fast food but wouldn't mind her somewhat tattered appearance. She needed comfort food – bad.

She walked into the converted Victorian home and was rather tentatively hailed by the sandy haired engineer she'd met on Friday at the reception.

"Good evening, Ms. Sherman. What a surprise to see you here tonight."

"Good evening to you, Dr. Balle. Are you alone? If so, please join me."

Caitlin thought for a minute. She'd met the engineer being dragged around by Pinkney. Perhaps she could find out what the little slime ball wanted. "As a matter of fact, I would like that."

She seated herself and the two women perused the menu.

"I have to be honest, I'm really not familiar with low country food. Perhaps you could guide me, Dr. Balle?"

Caitlin laughed. "Well, for starters, as I said Friday, please call me Caitlin. And we do have a taste for some unique things. A lot of our food traditions are based on what we can grow, hunt, or catch. I promise, I won't recommend anything lethal."

Amanda laughed. "Please do call me Amanda. I'm afraid I grew up in Ohio and was raised on a sustained diet of beef and potatoes, with the occasional fried catfish thrown in for variety."

"Oh, well, we will just have to educate your palate. For a starter, the mac and cheese is safest, but if you want to do a little adventuring, try the she-crab soup."

"She-crab?"

"Yup – they garnish and enrich it with crab eggs and sweet sherry."

"Sounds rich."

"And delicious."

"Okay, I'll experiment."

Caitlin laughed. "For Charlestonians, this isn't experimentation – it's just part of life! Want to keep experimenting?"

Amanda grinned. "If you recommend it, I'm game."

"Oh, this isn't a game dish. Proper fried chicken, drizzled with honey and served with hoppin' john and collard greens."

"What's hopping john?" Amanda asked rather flatly.

"Oh, it's the best rice and beans dish you'll ever eat – make N'orleans red beans and rice look sick."

Amanda just gave her a confused look.

"It's spicy black-eyed peas, cooked with smoked ham, and mixed with rice. It's delicious."

"What the hell! If I don't like it, Mickey D's is always open." Amanda laughed.

The two women placed their orders, with Caitlin

choosing fresh fish, and perloo with andouille sausage for herself.

The two women chatted politely about living in Charleston. The county board had found Amanda a furnished apartment in a huge old Victorian a couple of blocks north of Broadway and she'd wandered around the area finding nice little restaurants like Poogan's and the local museums, though her work kept her from visiting most of them.

Finally, during dessert of pecan pie and coffee, the conversation got to what Caitlin really wanted to know. "So, you were with Mr. Pinkney at the reception the other night. Can I ask what he's got you here to do?"

Amanda sighed. "He's got his heart set on building a community-oriented yacht club out at Hobcaw Point. There are a slew of potential problems there, but he's not listening. Come hell or high water, he wants to take advantage of what used to be a natural harbor and I'm pretty sure was a shipyard of some sort once upon a time. Now all there is left are a bunch of piling stubs, some old foundations for various buildings, and an old cemetery."

"So you're telling me it's more likely a historical site than a yacht club?"

"If I had to guess, yes. But Pinkney was at that reception to try and persuade the local history types to let him have his yacht club."

'Yeah, well, we will see about that,' Caitlin thought to herself. An idea started to form in her beady brain. "Unfortunately, Mr. Pinkney can be very persuasive when he wants to be. If it's truly a historic site, though, I'd hate to see it levelled."

"At least I can try to be careful to preserve what I can, and they can't do anything until we can get the family's permission to move the cemetery – if we can even find the family."

"Oh, in Charleston, I think you will be able to find the family with no trouble." She didn't bother to tell Amanda that she'd already found the family and that they were going to move that cemetery over her dead body.

CHAPTER 2

FIRST THING MONDAY MORNING, HENRY PINKNEY left a message for Amanda to see him in his office as soon as she got in.

"Mr. Pinkney, you wanted me?"

"Yes, yes, Amanda. I want you to get your crew together and start clearing Hobcaw Point as soon as possible. I have it on good authority that the property will officially be the county's within the next thirty days, and it will take you at least that long to have it cleared."

"Sir, I believe it is illegal to conduct any work on property that you do not own."

"Nonsense, woman. The county has the authority to clear any property that is abandoned and untended, regardless of ownership."

"Yes, sir. I will see to it."

Amanda trudged back to her office, pulled up a list of names and numbers on her computer, and started making phone calls. It was going to be a long, complicated week.

THE MUSEUM WAS CLOSED on Mondays, though the staff working on exhibits usually came in to work. Caitlin parked herself at the door of her family lawyer's office, which was conveniently just a two-block walk from her house. She had to wait. She knew she would, so had stopped on the way at Miller's for a cup of coffee. Finally, Mr. Spencer Rowe arrived, looking very surprised at the stressed looking young woman on his doorstep.

"Caitlin, to what do I owe this early morning visit? As far as I know, all of your father's affairs have been satisfactorily settled."

"Spencer, it's this." She handed him the document defining the county's eminent domain claim. "Henry Pinkney wants to build some sort of marina or yacht club out at Hobcaw Point. He claims that without an official deed, even though they have a record of our family paying property taxes every year for over a hundred years, the county can take it."

Spencer read through the documents, set them aside, and looked at Caitlin. "Well, we can at least slow the little worm down. Such a wanna be. Did you know that his father changed their name to Pinkney to try and be accepted into Charleston society? Shame he didn't know how to spell it correctly."

Spencer sucked on his cheeks for a few minutes, reading back through the papers. "Okay, I'll see what I can do to stop him. I can be quite annoying when I want to be. In the meantime, see if you can find that deed. Whatever you do, do not sign permission to move that cemetery, and perhaps your friends at the museum could put another kink in poor Henry's plans by declaring it a historical site."

"I will certainly try to find the deed – in fact, I've already started looking. You'd be amazed at how much old, useless paper I managed to pitch in the process. Father had every utility bill he'd ever received, all neatly filed. I pitched them." Both of them laughed. Stephen Balle had been notoriously anal retentive.

"And getting it declared a historical site?"

"Well, that's interesting. I'm working on an exhibit on life here before the Revolutionary War. Hobcaw's foundations go back to the early-1700s. Perhaps... perhaps Sarah will be interested."

"Well, dear, you see what you can do while I work on the legal end of things. Don't worry – one way or another, we can haul Henry's reins in."

"Wish he was more like a horse, rather than just being a horse's ass!"

"Oh, my dear, you insult the equine species."

They both chuckled, and Caitlin gathered her belongings.

"No, leave the paperwork with me. After all, I am your attorney. It's my job to deal with annoying paper."

"Thank you, Spencer. I don't know what I'd do without you."

The silver haired attorney laughed again. "I'm a little old for you, dear – and I suspect the wrong gender."

Caitlin's eyes grew as round as saucers. "You think I'm...?"

"Caitlin, I've known you since you were eight years old. Of course, I know. I hope you find a charming woman to be your companion. I promise I will not do what your mother does and start introducing you to eligible women. I figure you can handle that part all by yourself.""

Caitlin hugged the older man good bye.

"Be careful, Caitlin. I'll keep you posted on the legal issues."

She chose to walk from his office to work, a pleasant twenty-minute walk that would give her time to think about how to approach Sarah with the idea of declaring Hobcaw a historical site.

SARAH HIGHSMITH HAD NOT BEEN in the office on Monday, so Caitlin had worked on her plans for the colonial life exhibit. That evening, she started in on the next phase of her search for the deed.

She devoted a chunk of Monday night going through the books and ledgers on the shelves in the library cum den at her home. She found plenty of fascinating things – invoices for materials for the shipyard, bills of sale from the merchant ships built at the yard, commissions for work during the Civil War, records related to the maintenance of the shipyard and the town house – but no deed. Most of what she found was related to the 1800s. She needed to find the earlier sections of the library.

Tuesday morning saw Caitlin trudging into work early, hoping to catch Sarah before she went back to the site she was working on out on Sullivan's Island. If she was going to get Hobcaw declared a historic site, she had to act quickly, as the paperwork was painful. As a starting point, she created a rough sketch of the Hobcaw site, showing generally the location of each of the remaining foundations and the functions of the buildings they had once supported.

When Sarah arrived, Caitlin was waiting for her. "I have a thought, and I hope you'll find it interesting. As you know, I'm working on the colonial life exhibit. Well, we have a site in the county here that has not been explored but was an active shipyard throughout the 1700s and on until it was destroyed during the Civil War. There are a number of building foundations, and I suspect that there's a wealth of information we could harvest from the site." She pulled the sketch of the site out to show it to Sarah.

"Uh huh. This wouldn't happen to be the site that Pinkney wants to turn into a marina – excuse me – yacht club?"

"Ah, yes."

"And you wouldn't happen to have a personal interest in the site, would you? Is that how you know so much about it?"

"Um, well, actually, it's been in my family for about 350 years, so, yes, I have an interest. But more importantly, it's a part of Charleston history and I'd hate to see a marina built over it. Not to mention that it was the first shipyard in Charleston. It was lived on since around 1680 and a shipyard all through the 1700s and up until 1865. While Sherman spared Charleston, he did put the torch to the family's shipyard because of the role we had played in keeping the blockade busters going."

Sarah laughed. "I've already started the research. You and I have a mutual friend. Spencer is one of the men my mother used to throw me at. It didn't take rocket science to figure out that the historical site Spencer was talking about is the same one you want to protect AND is the one that Mr. Pinkney without a "C" wants to turn into a yacht club, preferably named after him. Want to go out and walk the site on Friday with me?"

"I'd be very grateful if you would look at it."

"Wear boots Friday." Sarah grinned, grabbed her kit bag of tools, and walked out the door.

ON WEDNESDAY MORNING, a semi hauled a trailer onto the Hobcaw Point site. They cleared and levelled the ground, then settled the trailer on the site that would serve as the headquarters for the activities to be conducted. That afternoon, trucks from the electric company and the phone company came and hooked up the utilities for the trailer, raising a couple of poles to reach the lines running along Hobcaw Drive to support the cluster of houses across the street. Late that afternoon, a smaller truck deposited two porta-potties on the ground. On Thursday, crews from the county were scheduled to come in with a backhoe and hook up the water and sewer lines from the road to the trailer. By Friday, it would be ready for Amanda to move her office in and her staff on-site. In the meantime, a crew began cutting down the long grasses and shrubs that populated the area, moving towards the little harbor.

The old man sat on his stone and watched all this activity, scowling at the interlopers.

"Tiernan, Quinn, Birch, Grear, Kade. I need you."

The summoned entities assembled quietly, standing before the old man. "You called, Laird?"

Tiernan was almost as old looking as the Laird, with baggy brown clothes, a scruffy beard, and the faint aroma of Irish whiskey radiating off him. At his side was a dark boy with gentle hazel eyes, black hair, and clothed in what looked like a collection of moss and leaves. Tiny Grear and Kade settled their brown selves on a couple of rocks in front of the Laird. The last member of the troop finally strolled up, puffing on his pipe that somehow never seemed to burn out.

"Ah, Quinn, so you did choose to join us."

"Aye. What has you so excited after all these years? I hae not seen you so since that Yankee scum burned the shipyard?"

"There be people coming to make changes – changes I nae want or like, I be thinking. I want ye to find out who they are and what they are trying to do. And I want ye to slow them down as much as ye can."

Ciara had been leaning out of her tree to listen to the old man. Her eyes glowed brilliant red. "Laird, I shall do what I can to scare the livers out of them."

"I am sure you will, my dear. Just see that ye dinna wail for one of ours."

"Nay, Laird, yours are safe for a while yet. Stephen was the last."

The troop of Fae gathered together under the old oak to start planning their strategy for harassing the intruders. If the humans working around the trailer could have heard their laughter as they schemed, they would have shivered in fear.

Quinn turned back to the Laird, who was still sitting on

his stone, talking with the mistress, who had joined him while they were plotting. "My Laird, what of Ronan? Surely there will be things in the sea to make their tasks more difficult."

"Good point, little man. I shall have a word with our skin shedder anon."

BIRCH, who was what the Scots called a Ghillie Dhu – a dark boy – watched the workers cutting down the bushes and young trees using loud, smoke-spouting machines they called bush hogs. Birch wondered what he could do to foul those spinning blades that brought death to the sprouts of pine and oak that had become his children during the many years he had roamed this sandy land.

As he watched, the men using the bush hogs ran into a patch of a vine called Virginia creeper that was wrapped around some of the bushes they were hacking down. The tough, wiry, and persistent vine wrapped around the blades, not being cut, but instead binding around the rotating blades as if they were a reel meant to hold the tough tendrils. The result was abrupt; the bush hogs stopped cold. It gave Birch an idea.

As he watched the men try to cut away the tenacious tendrils, he noticed they were wearing shorts as a hedge against the hot weather. A small smirk graced his lips as he thought of another of his flora-based friends. Poison ivy would make a lovely garnish to the damage the Virginia creeper would do.

Grear and Kade watched attentively while the men from

the electric company hooked cables to the box on the side of the trailer. They paid careful attention as the men stripped the ends of the different colored wires and screwed them into the appropriate terminals, being careful not to let the ends touch one another. Grear whispered to Kade, "Darlin', you take the black ones and I'll take the red ones. Shall we see what happens when the wires touch?"

Instead of focusing on the surrounds, Quinn watched the workers themselves. "Hummm. Boots, short pants, gloves. Now, how many ways can I make these boys miserable?"

As the sun sank into the west, the workers stowed their equipment and went into the trailer, emerging a little while later dressed, for the most part, in jeans, running shoes, and clean shirts.

"Ah, here's an opportunity for a good old cobbler to practice his trade – or unpractice it as the case may be."

Once the trailer was empty, Quinn slipped in and found the lockers where the workmen had stashed their clothes. He pulled the first pair of boots out, looking at them with the critical eye of a good cobbler. He slid the insole out of the boot and carefully scraped the leather under where the ball of the workman's foot rested until it was paper thin. He then replaced the insole. On the other boot, he loosened the grip of the glue that held the sole together, and snipped some of the threads that reinforced the meld of boot and sole. He figured one way or the other, this pair of boots would give out by mid-afternoon. He performed similar surgery on every pair of workman's boots in the trailer. He then looked at the work gloves stashed in the lockers, and weakened stitches, enhanced any cracks in the leather, and wore thin spots until they were ready to break through.

While Quinn was playing with leather, Birch was talking quietly with his friends in the forest. To the Virginia creeper, he encouraged them to embrace every bush and sprout they could find. He asked the foliage to support this intruder they normally tried to avoid, as the creeper could protect them from the evil blades. He turned to the poison ivy and invited them to lay down a carpet of soft, slightly fuzzy tri-leafed stems that would protect the delicate roots of young sprouts within the forest. As he talked, other plants in the community, including both poison oak and poison sumac, volunteered to participate as well. Particularly eager to help were the Cenchrus grass – better known as sandspurs. If a plant could have an evil grin, Cenchrus did.

Grear and Kade spent some time surveying the globe with the spinning platter attached to the side of the trailer. Finally, Kade carefully pulled out the pin that held the door on the bottom of the contraption in place and dropped the flap door. Inside, they found the heavy cable from the road attached to a black block with three cables; one was white, one was black, and one was red, and each had a small end of raw copper ending in a terminal on the black block. The two brownies looked at one another, and then started gnawing at the colored woven fiber covers on the copper leads. Eventually, they had removed enough of the insulation so they could twist the three wires together. After a brief shower of sparks, the platter stopped spinning. Smiling to themselves, they resealed the door.

At the first sign of the coming dawn, all five of the Fae

members of the Laird's troops reported to the old man sitting on his stone. "It has started, sir."

"Good, good. Let us see what your handiwork does to their plans."

Siobhan sat on her stone, looking at the satisfied mischief makers. "I trust you hurt no one."

"Nae, mistress – at least not in any way that will cause long-term harm. Wet and sandy feet, the odd blister, some welts from the poison ivy – that is the extent of the current damage."

"Well, let us see what our little annoyances do to their activities. For now, let us just keep watch."

THURSDAY MORNING WAS a bit of a nightmare for Amanda. She came into the office and hit the button to boot up her computer. Nothing. She tried to turn on the lamp over her drawing table. Nothing. She realized that the air conditioner wasn't pumping cool air into what was otherwise a perfect sun oven.

"Oh, crap. The electric company was just here yesterday. Everything was working last night. Damn, damn, damn." She picked up the phone to call the utility, and cursed some more as there was no dial tone. Reaching for her briefcase, she dug out her cell phone and started making the necessary calls.

The crew members came in and started pulling on their work gear in the locker room, cursing right along with Amanda over the lack of power and specifically the lack of air conditioning. With just a few more grumbles, they wandered out to continue the massive job of hacking back the undergrowth that had taken over much of the Point.

Both of the hand-guided bush hogs fouled within an hour of starting work. The Virginia creeper was doing a spectacular job of tangling in the blades and embedding its tendrils in the gears that drove them. While struggling with the annoying vines, one of the workers pulled off his gloves to be able to get to the tangled mess around the drive gear. He then absentmindedly scratched his leg above his sock, then slapped at a mosquito on his cheek. Within minutes, an itchy red rash appeared on his cheek, matching the rash that was crawling up his leg.

"Fucking hell!" yelled one of the other workers. "Poison ivy."

The foreman handed one of the workmen a couple of twenty-dollar bills. "Run over to the CVS and get some cortisone cream and calamine lotion." The man took off immediately, jogging toward his truck. "And don't forget to bring me the receipt," the foreman yelled after him.

Within a half hour, the men were slathering various parts of their anatomies with cortisone cream and cursing softly. "Tomorrow, please wear long pants," the foreman said resignedly.

He wandered over to the trailer and found Amanda sitting under a nearby tree, looking relatively miserable as she waited in Charleston's muggy summer heat for the utility company to show up. "Um, Miss Amanda?"

She looked up, and seeing his miserable expression, she knew he was the bearer of more bad news. "Well, both of our bush hogs are fouled with vines and the men have found a vicious patch of poison ivy."

As he talked, one of the men came limping back to the trailer, sat down on the steps, and pulled his boots and socks off.

The foreman yelled, "Jake, what's wrong?"

The man answered with one word as he patiently began picking the wicked little burrs off his socks and boots. "Sandspurs."

Amanda sank her head into her hands.

"If this keeps up, it'll take us twice as long as we estimated to clear the land."

Amanda's head sank even lower.

The utility guys finally showed up at four in the afternoon. They opened the switch box and saw the damage that had been done. It only took a few minutes to trim, re-strip, and reconnect the wires. "Looks like squirrels got into the box last night. Sometimes they like to chew on the insulation, so I put a lock on the box. You have electricity back."

"Thank you, gentlemen. I appreciate it."

As the electric company men were loading up, the foreman of the water company crew came stomping up. "We're sorry, Ms. Sherman, but it's taking us longer than we expected. We keep running into roots that have to be cut. We'll be back in the morning to finish up."

Amanda nodded. "Of course. I doubt anything on this site is going to be simple."

"Well, ma'am, see you tomorrow." With that, he walked off, shaking his head at the annoyances his men had encountered all day.

Kade whispered to Grear, "Sherman? Oh, the Laird is not going to be happy."

"The last Sherman to come through here burned everything to the ground. I wonder what this one will do."

"If it is up to us, she shall do naught to Hobcaw Point."

"Except perhaps clear out the weeds – slowly!" The two brownies chuckled.

They quietly crept back to the old oak tree beside the cemetery as the last of the work crew gathered their belongings and headed home for the night.

Amanda looked around once more before she climbed in the old Jeep. She had the oddest feeling that she was somehow being watched.

"HER NAME IS WHAT?" Samuel leapt from his stone, bellowing in anger and frustration. "Another of that cursed family is here to further damage our beloved land?"

"Now, husband," Siobhan spoke soothingly. "She is not her ancestor, if indeed he is her ancestor at all. Sherman is not all that an uncommon name."

"And if she is his ill-begotten get? If she is a member of that God-be-damned family? They burned my shipyard and home to the ground! What if she is here to do yet more damage to my legacy?"

"Let us wait to see what her intentions are. You know that it is best to know your enemy before you act. So will we keep close and keep good counsel."

Samuel settled back onto his stone, arms crossed across his chest and an intense pout planted firmly on his bearded face. "For now. But if she is the product of that scum, I make no promises."

Siobhan just gently stroked his shoulder.

FRIDAY MORNING CAME with a haze over the sky, crushing humidity, and more heat than usual for so early in the day. Amanda sighed as she opened the trailer, and was welcomed by working air conditioning. With the knowledge that there was poison ivy on the grounds, she had worn canvas pants and high-topped boots to work today.

Promptly at eight, the water and sewer crew arrived and continued their laborious task of laying pipe to the office trailer. Fortunately, it would eventually be replaced by one of the buildings for the yacht club, so it was not a temporary task.

Birch watched from the nearest stand of oaks as the back hoe, supported by men with axes, dug through the roots that fed his beloved trees. He glanced at the collection of sprouts behind him, sprouts he would plant that evening along the sides of the ditches. The weeping willows' roots would seek out the water lines and would find every crack and joint in the pipes. While it would not provide instant relief from the invasion of his domain, they would do the job of debilitating the pipes with relatively prompt efficiency.

Shortly after the ditch diggers had started their day, the surveying team showed up, clad in safety vests and bright yellow safari hats, and hauling their various pieces of gear over to the trailer. They dropped their poles and tripods in a pile by the door while setting down more delicate gear like the theodolites and prisms more gently.

"Good morning, folks. Come in and I'll show you the

map I've set up for you to do your charting." The four-person crew crammed into the room at one end of the trailer where Amanda had her drawing table. They peered at her site map, nodding as they discussed the importance of finding and mapping all the remaining foundations on the property, as the stonework could be hell on equipment once the work began if it were not properly identified.

While Amanda was talking with the surveyors, the ground crew showed up, some painted with calomel lotion, and all wearing thick pants and heavy boots, and griping mightily about having to wear heavy clothes in hot, muggy weather. The foreman stopped the team in the locker room to plan the day's work. "Gentlemen, with the amount of Virginia creeper out there, I think it might be better to use the metal blade weed whackers. At least the damned vines won't foul the gears."

Amanda took a moment away from her conversation with the surveyors. "Because the dredging guys are due on Monday, could you folks clear the area around the harbor today, please?"

The crew groaned. The harbor was surrounded by mud flats and saw grass – the toughest grass they ever had to deal with. What was worse was the edges of the blades were sharp little buggers – they could leave a collection of cuts like paper cuts – and just as painful. The men grabbed their gloves and trooped out to collect the whackers, check the blades, and start hacking at the miserable sedge surrounding the old harbor. The mud flats made using the bush hogs impossible.

Amanda turned back to the surveyors, who were starting to get their gear unpacked and set up. One of them was cursing under her breath. Amanda looked at her, questioning, "What's wrong?"

"Oh, the compass seems to be picking up something magnetized. It won't settle. Without a reliable compass reading, we will have some real problems."

"Perhaps it's something in the trailer or with the guys' equipment."

"I'll try it out at different places around the property. Otherwise, I'll need to go back to the office to get one that is working correctly."

"Could you use your GPS device in its place?"

"I could, but that will present other calculating problems. We'll figure out a way to make it work."

"Let me know if you have any more problems or if I can help somehow."

They nodded and started hiking across the property.

Amanda retreated into the welcoming coolness of the trailer and wandered into the kitchenette, hoping to find a coffee machine. She was disappointed. All she found were some Styrofoam cups, a few individual packets of instant coffee, powdered creamer, sugar packets, and her least favorite artificial sweetener. She shrugged. She needed the caffeine. The water cooler in the corner also provided semi-hot water. With a shrug, she opened a packet, added creamer and a sugar, filled the cup with water, stirred till the lumps dissolved, and grimaced as she sipped the tepid concoction.

A loud knock on the trailer door interrupted her brief moment of peace. "Oh bloody hell, what now?" she mumbled to herself.

Opening the door, she was stunned to see the already

sweaty, slightly pink and definitely pudgy face of Henry Pinkney.

"Good morning, Amanda. I just stopped by to see how things are going on our little project."

"Come in, Mr. Pinkney. The groundsmen are working away, though they have run into several problems. The undergrowth is denser than your report suggested—just some of the issues that always plague a project start up."

"So, show me what you're doing to get going."

"Certainly, sir." She put down the cup of the sorry excuse for caffeine and pulled her hat and sun glasses on. "Let's take a walk so I can show you how we've started."

She led the man down toward the old harbor, where the crew was slowly working their way through the saw grass. "We're clearing the shore to prepare for the dredging crew."

As they walked toward the water, they stepped into one of the mud flats. Henry Pinkney felt his woven leather Italian loafers sink into the muck. Each step he took made an unpleasant sucking sound. It only took three steps before his socks were soaking wet.

Amanda pointed to the team of people wading through brush on the bank of Hobcaw Creek. "The surveyors have begun the detailed mapping, and checking for all remnants of building foundations to refine the plot map for the site. It is crucial that they identify all remaining foundation ruins or we could have a serious problem with damage to equipment when we start preparing the site for buildings, roads, parking areas and such." She turned to walk back up toward the trailer. "As you can see, the water department is laying the lines from up off of Hobcaw Drive to bring water and sewer services to a central point for future distribution. They're having a bit of a time getting through the tree roots, though."

As she talked, Pinkney grunted at appropriate points, not really understanding a thing she was saying, in part because he really didn't understand and in part because he was more concerned with what the mud was doing to his ridiculously expensive Santoni loafers. He was also concerned about telling her that she might have to slow down her work because that eternally annoying, snooty, condescending, snobbish attorney Spencer Rowe had filed a bunch of motions with the circuit court that complicated the whole process of taking ownership of the property from the Balle family.

"Ah, good, good, Amanda. I knew we had the right person for this project when we hired you."

'Right person my ass. What made me right for this, twerp, was the price,' she thought.

Before she could actually say anything, he continued on. "It is just as well that there are additional challenges, as we have run into a little complication with the courts. You may be getting some visits from lawyers and such, so I wanted you to be prepared."

'Uh oh. The family has found out about using injunctions to disrupt eminent domain claims.' Amanda felt a little bit of satisfaction that the smarmy little jerk was getting some push back. 'Maybe I better look for another site for this guy's yacht club fantasy.' She just smiled at Pinkney and said, "I will, of course, cooperate however I can."

As they came up to the trailer, yet another vehicle pulled into the area they were using for parking. This time it was an older gray-green Range Rover. Amanda grinned for a moment – that car was everything her Jeep wished it could be.

Two women climbed out of the vehicle and strolled toward the trailer. Amanda's grin remained. Not only was the vehicle everything it should be, both women were properly dressed for stomping around this property. They had on boots with canvas pants tucked into them, and long-sleeved light-colored shirts. They also wore wide brimmed hats and sun glasses. Certainly, they were better dressed for the Point than Pinkney, in his fancy loafers and expensive suit that Amanda noticed was now decorated with a collection of sandspurs up to his knees.

Pinkney muttered under his breath, but Amanda couldn't tell what he was saying. He put a patently false smile on his face and offered his hand to the women as they walked up to join them. "Drs. Highsmith and Balle, to what do we owe the pleasure of your company this morning?"

Caitlin responded sharply, "Why, Mr. Pinkney, is there a law preventing me from visiting my own property? At least while it's still mine."

"Of course not, Dr. Balle. I understand that you suggest this is a historic site, though that has yet to be determined." Pinkney's defenses were obviously up.

"Indeed, Mr. Pinkney," Sarah Highsmith almost purred at him. "That's what the court has asked me to determine."

"Isn't that a little convenient for you, Dr. Balle – your boss is who the court asked to do the evaluation?"

"Actually, Mr. Pinkney, Joselyn O'Malley, the Chief of Collections, is my boss. The curators have very little interaction with the Archaeology Department at the Museum." Caitlyn smiled sweetly at the blustering man.

According to Mr. Rowe, the judge saw no conflict, especially considering Dr. Highsmith's reputation."

"Well, you do what you must, and I'll do what I must. Good day, ladies." With that, Pinkney huffed over to his Cadillac, gunned the motor, and roared off down the oyster shell road.

CHAPTER 3

AMANDA TURNED TO THE TWO WOMEN WHO HAD been left standing, staring at the dust cloud Pinkney had left behind. "Would you like to come into the office? I'm afraid all I can offer is some bad instant coffee, but we could talk about what you want here."

They climbed into the trailer, but declined bad coffee.

"So, Drs. Balle and Highsmith, what can I do for you?"

Sarah spoke first. "For starters, you can call me Sarah. I think we will be seeing a good bit of one another in the next few weeks and months."

"And I am Amanda, please."

"Okay, now that we have that settled, as you know, Pinkney wants to turn this property into some kind of community yacht club. We think he's using some underhanded legal actions to take the property for the county for one, and we suspect you've got a pretty interesting historical site here. Hobcaw Point was the first shipyard in Charleston. It played a role in the Revolution.

the War of 1812, and the Civil War. So, even if Caitlin can't keep the title to this land, we think the Historical Society can stop Henry Pinkney from his little delusion of grandeur." Sarah paused for a moment. "Are you willing to help us?"

Amanda took a deep breath, looking at both women carefully.

Before she could say anything, Caitlin broke in. "My family has owned this property since the late 1600s. It functioned as a shipyard until 1865, when Sherman's troops burned it down after they destroyed Columbia. That little wannabe keeps trying to find ways to link himself to the old Charleston families. This is just another one of his half-assed attempts to do so."

"I noticed that his name isn't spelled the same way the famous family does theirs. I assume that is an error?"

"His father had the same ambitions – so he changed their name. Shame he didn't know how to spell it."

All three women laughed.

Amanda went on. "I am also sorry my great-great-great-grandfather did such damage to your family. I do hope you don't hold it against me."

They heard a small twitter that sounded like it came from the corner. Amanda grinned. "Don't worry – we have some, um, persistent squirrels around here."

Sarah joined the conversation. "It takes some doing to have a property declared historically protected. However, with the right information, I think we can do it. I saw you've got surveyors working the property. Can you make sure they document every single remaining foundation on the plat?"

"Of course, I can."

"Good. The more foundations that are identified, the more we have to work with."

Amanda looked at the two women thoughtfully. "I am trained as a civil engineer – a tough job for anyone and especially for a woman. They hired me because I'm young and, bluntly, because I'm cheap. A nice yacht club in my portfolio would help my career enormously, but a reconstructed historical site would be a much better qualification. I will help. Hopefully, you can help me when the site is declared protected and we want to do something for the public with it." She thought for a few minutes. "I need to do a sounding of the harbor and creek, too. This may not be a good site for what Pinkney wants anyway. I'm not sure the creek will support the keel depths for modern sail boats – it's silted up pretty badly, and the little sand bar island over there has grown considerably in the past hundred years."

Sarah looked off into space for a minute. "Perhaps you should have your surveyors take a look at the part of the property that faces the Wando River. That may make a much better yacht club. Caitlin, is it part of the family property?"

"I'm pretty sure some of it is, but I need to find the damned deed to be sure. And I think Spencer is having his folks pull the old plat maps from the tax records."

Sarah smiled. "That will help – both in assisting Amanda with making recommendations for the yacht club and in establishing the extent of your holdings here."

The three women spent the next several hours walking the property and examining the various foundations that were still visible. Of particular interest to Sarah were the ruins of the smithy, the main house, and what she suspected had been a dry dock. She also worked her way through the original family cemetery with great interest.

As she finished up some notes on the site, Sarah looked at the two other women with a grin on her face. "If this turns out the way I think it will, we may be able to find some money to reconstruct at least the important parts of the site. I'm thinking sort of like what they've done up at Jamestown. What do you think?"

Caitlin looked at her with her mouth hanging open. "You mean make it into a real historical site? What about my ownership?"

"It could be a grant supported money maker, if you want."

"I would need to think about that – and get Pinkney off on another hair-brained scheme."

"Well, you think about it. I'll see if there is any money rolling around for such a thing."

They walked back to the trailer. Sarah turned to Caitlin. "Listen, I need to run over to Sullivan's Island for a bit. You can come with me, if you want."

Amanda cleared her throat. "I could run you back into town, if you prefer. They don't need me on site this afternoon."

Caitlin grinned. "Seems I'm pretty popular today. If you don't mind, Sarah, I'll take Amanda's offer. Shall I see you in the office tomorrow?"

"Oh, yes, you certainly will. We need to talk about getting sites on the National Register."

"Yes, ma'am. We'll be good little historians tomorrow.

Today, I want to rid my socks of sandspurs and put on something a little more appropriate to the weather."

Sarah laughed and waved goodbye as she walked to her Rover.

Caitlin turned to Amanda. "Since it's already late afternoon and we all missed lunch, can I invite you to an early dinner? We can continue your education in low country cuisine, if you'd like."

"I can certainly stand to have some food, and your company is most enlightening, Caitlin. I'd be honored to attend another lesson."

"Good. Tell me you like seafood."

"Depends on the seafood. I like shrimp and lobster, and most fish. I have to confess, I'm a little hesitant to try raw oysters, though I've seen them all over town."

Caitlin laughed. "We're breaking you into low country cooking slowly, oh, you midwestern Yankee."

"I'm game for whatever you want."

"Well, first I want a shower and some clean clothes."

"Me too. Shall we hit my place first, then yours? That way, no backtracking."

"Oh, we'll be backtracking today, but you'll see."

They piled into Amanda's Jeep and headed through Mt. Pleasant toward the river.

"All right, take the Cooper River Bridge into town, then to your place."

"Isn't that the Ravenel Bridge?"

"Yes, but we don't usually use that name."

"Why not?"

"Well, this bridge replaced the old ones, and Mr. Ravenel has, how shall we say, a number of people who don't admire him very much and didn't think the bridge should be named for him."

"And you're one of those people?"

"Oh, you could say that." She thought for a minute. "Ravenel made Governor Wallace look liberal."

"Oh," came out flat and a little cold. "I understand now."

They chatted about the landmarks they drove by until they reached Amanda's apartment building. She pulled around to the side, where parking was available for the residents. The two got out of the car and walked up one floor to Amanda's apartment, which had a living room that had once been a parlor, a kitchenette with the basic utilities, and Caitlin assumed a bedroom and bath. "Not bad for a furnished place."

"Yes, it's actually very comfortable. The A/C works well, thank the Goddess."

Caitlin grinned. "Charleston is pretty difficult without A/C. My grandfather had central air installed in my house back in the 50's. I bless his memory every May."

"There's juice and water in the fridge. Help yourself. I won't be long, and what is appropriate dress for this place we're going to?"

"Shorts, sandals, and a shirt you don't mind getting messy."

"Messy?"

"Yes, messy. People have a tendency to drip butter on themselves with what I have in mind."

Amanda laughed. "I'm good at dripping butter." She chuckled as she disappeared into the bedroom.

Caitlin retrieved a bottle of water and stood at the window looking out over the back yard, which the owners had maintained as a garden for their tenants. She considered the possibility of the engineer actually helping her rather than being loyal to Pinkney.

She strolled over to the bookshelf beside the fireplace in the parlor and glanced at the pictures that had been set on the shelves in front of the books that obviously came with the apartment – guidebooks, Charleston history, and the like. More than one was obviously of Amanda and her parents, as well as a young man who was, from his resemblance to the engineer, her brother. He was slightly taller, lanky, and sandy-haired. They looked very much alike. There was also a picture of Amanda with her arm around a lovely brunette, a woman who was obviously no relation but who, from the embrace and the looks on both faces, was clearly someone she was very close with. 'Hummm. I wonder if she's family. Sure looks like it.'

Amanda came through the door to her room very quietly and saw Caitlin holding the picture of herself with Anna, who had been her lover through the last year of undergraduate school and the first year of her master's work. Anna couldn't handle Amanda's need to move with the work, and chose to return to her home town and her high school sweetheart. It had been six years since they parted, and they had remained good friends. In fact, Amanda was godmother to Anna and Charlene's first-born child.

"She's my ex. Couldn't handle the constant moving. We're still friends, but that's all." Amanda held her breath, waiting for Caitlin's response.

Caitlin grinned. "Her loss. If you love someone, you can find ways to make it work." She sat the picture back on the shelf. "So, can we go relieve me of this layer of sweat, sand, and muck?"

"Only if you tell me I'm properly dressed for dinner."

Caitlin looked up and down at her companion and smiled. The lean form topped with jaw length sandy hair and the deeply tanned skin were nicely set off by the blue cotton short-sleeved shirt. Nicely muscled legs emerged from a pair of khaki walking shorts and slender feet were wrapped in the straps of a pair of flat sandals. All in all, she looked... delicious. Caitlin mentally shook herself. This was not the time to let her hormones take control. "You look perfect for where I plan to take us. You'll fit right in. Shall we go to my place so I can fit in too?"

Amanda glanced around her little apartment, somehow a little sad that it showed so little of her personality. It was one of the prices of moving from place to place. She closed and locked the door and followed Caitlin down the stairs.

It only took a few minutes to get to Caitlin's house. "You can pull into the driveway beside the house. We'll only be a few minutes."

Caitlin led the way into the house through the side door, which opened into the kitchen. "Help yourself to whatever is in the fridge; we're about thirty minutes from the restaurant I'm taking you to. And look around. The house was built at the end of the 1600s and has been upgraded and added to repeatedly since then. I'll be back down in a jiff."

As the red-head tromped up the stairs in her heavy boots, Amanda looked around. The doors were low, as was typical for old houses, but the ceilings were high – twelve feet if they were an inch – and the windows were set to let air in – a defense against the heat and humidity that plagued

Charleston in the summer. There were fireplaces in each room that Amanda could see, but the room that drew her attention was a classic 17th century library that was furnished as an office. Windows faced the side yard, and a fireplace covered part of one wall. The rest of the room was a combination of built-in shelves reaching to the ceiling and inset windows to allow a breeze through the room. The woodwork was exquisite and somehow gave more depth to the window insets than she would have expected.

As she stepped over to look more closely at the bookcases, Caitlin appeared at the door, her hair still damp and flowing down her back. Like Amanda, she was dressed in shorts, a light weight shirt, and open toed sandals.

"You ready to—"

She was interrupted by the phone ringing.

"Hello?" She paused. "Hello, Mother." Another pause. "No, I don't. I was just going out to dinner with a friend." Pause. "No. She's the engineer I met at the reception last week. I'm introducing her to low-country cuisine." Longer pause. After each pause, Caitlin's voice grew sharper. "Mother, drop it. I am not going to marry ANY man. This is not a phase I'm going through. I have a good career and good friends and I am perfectly capable of taking care of myself." Very long pause. "No, we will not discuss this again. I have to go; Amanda is waiting for me."

Caitlin hung up the phone, shaking her head and muttering to herself, though Amanda could not hear what she was saying. Then she took a deep breath and turned to her guest. "I'm sorry you had to hear that. Shall we go?"

"Yes, certainly. Lead the way."

They went back out the kitchen door, and after Caitlin

locked up, piled back into Amanda's Jeep. "Where to, ma'am?"

"Back over the bridge to Mt. Pleasant, to start with."

For the first few minutes of their drive, Caitlin was silent. Amanda gave her the space she obviously needed. As they neared the end of the bridge, Amanda asked, "Where to now?"

"Take the right-hand ramp onto Coleman Boulevard. When we cross the bridge ahead, you'll take the next right. Where we're going is right on Shem Creek."

Amanda drove on, following Caitlin's instructions. As they turned off Coleman on to Mill Street, Caitlin told her to take the next right as well. Ahead of them on the right was the parking lot for Red's Ice House.

"Is this the place?"

Caitlin nodded, then shook herself. After all, she had invited Amanda to dinner. Being the silent, sullen woman her mother inspired her to be wasn't fair to Amanda. "So, are you ready to face another low-country tradition?"

"Ready and willing. I'm starving."

"Good, 'cause the dinner I'm ordering for us is huge!"

"Lead on, then."

They entered Red's Ice House, with Amanda looking around, fascinated by the rough environment that obviously supplied fishermen, boaters and locals of various sorts. The tables and chairs were outside, protected from the sky by translucent panels and with tarps rolled up that could be lowered in the case of rain. Now a gentle breeze blew off the water of Shem Creek, protecting the diners from mosquitos and making the temperature tolerable.

They were seated at a corner table right beside the railing

looking over the creek. Evidently, Caitlin was known to the staff; they made an effort to provide her with the most comfortable location.

Amanda read the menu, seeing a number of things that were completely unfamiliar to her, a few things she didn't think she would ever eat, and very few things that looked safe. She looked up at Caitlin and said, "I'm clueless. I am completely at your mercy."

Caitlin laughed softly. "I promise, I won't offend you as long as shrimp and crabs are acceptable foods."

"Entirely acceptable."

Caitlin waved a server over and asked for some pimento cheese spread with captain wafers, a small pitcher of draft beer, and two low-country boils with crab. "You can bring me a half dozen oysters on the half shell with both sauces, too. And save a couple of key lime pies for us."

The waitress left, and Caitlin looked at Amanda with a serious and rather apologetic look on her face. "I'm truly sorry for subjecting you to that interaction with my mother, and for my sulking for the past half hour. I promise to be more social for the rest of the evening."

"I have some idea of what your mother is putting you through. My mother thought it was a phase as well. She's finally coming to realize it's not a phase, but just who I am. If you want to talk about it, I'm a good listener."

The waitress appeared with a pitcher of beer that was dripping with sweat and a small platter with a bowl of orange cheese with pieces of red liberally scattered through it and a pile of rectangular crackers, along with some sliced celery and sliced red bell peppers. She slid the tray onto the table and filled two frosted mugs from the pitcher she then left on the table.

Caitlin reached across the table and patted Amanda's hand. "I appreciate your thoughtfulness. Perhaps..."

"You've brought me into your problems with Pinkney. You can keep the trend going, if you want. I saw your mother at the reception. I would think being able to blow off steam would be a good thing."

Caitlin laughed at that while spreading some of the cheese on a cracker. "Okay. I'll talk. But first, try the pimento cheese. I promise, you'll love it." With that, she stuffed the loaded cracker in her mouth and chewed happily.

Amanda spread the cheese on a cracker and bit into it. Her eyebrows raised as a surprised look came over her face. She hadn't expected the heat, as it looked like a normal soft cheese spread. "Damn, that's good. What's in it?"

"It's sharp cheddar, cream cheese, a little mayo, garlic, onion, cayenne, jalapeno, and diced pimentos. Some people use cottage cheese instead of cream cheese. And it makes great sandwiches, too."

"I'm sure it does." Amanda stuffed another cheese laden cracker into her mouth.

Just then, the waitress appeared with a platter containing Caitlin's oysters. She speared one of the mollusks with the small fork, dipped it in the mignonette sauce, and slurped it down. The next one went into the cocktail sauce, and she chewed and swallowed that with a groan that was almost sexual.

Amanda grinned. "Okay, if they are that good, maybe I should try one."

"I thought you might." She swirled an oyster in the cocktail sauce and handed it over to Amanda.

Amanda looked at the small blob of what looked like mucus coated with red cocktail sauce, trying to gather courage to try the alien food form. "Just suck it in?"

"Suck it in, chew it, savor the lovely briny flavor, and swallow it down. Generations of people have been eating these things – how do you think they got all those shells that pave our roads?"

Amanda scrunched up her eyes, took a deep breath, and sucked in the chunk of meat. She chewed, carefully at first, then eagerly, before she swallowed. "Damn, that's good!"

"Oh, would you like some more?"

"Not right now, but some evening we have go pig out at an oyster bar."

"That can be arranged, Ms. Sherman."

Amanda went back to working her way through the pimento cheese, alternating between the vegetables and the crackers as the carriers. "Okay, so what is with your mother?"

"Well, for over 300 years, there have been Balles living in the Charleston area. Unfortunately, the family line has died down or moved away over the years, so I am the only Balle of my generation in the area. Which makes me the heir to the family heritage. There's always been a lot of pressure on me to marry and continue the family line." She sighed and took a swig of her beer.

"There's an obvious problem with that. I'm a lesbian, as I assume you figured out. The probability of me having a little Balle to carry on the line is slim to none."

"You know that's not true. If you want a child, artificial

insemination is easily arranged." Amanda gently patted Caitlin's hand.

"Oh, I know, but the idea of raising a child alone is just not something I'm willing to do. I'd need a partner who would be willing to commit to me, my child, and our bloody heritage. You got any hot ideas?" Caitlin laughed, a little harshly.

"Caitlin, you are a beautiful woman, charming, intelligent, with a great sense of humor. Surely, you'll find someone..."

That got a derisive snort from Caitlin. "Oh, how little you know. My mother has managed to drive away every woman I've ever been involved with, either by threatening, coercing, or bribing them. You know, there are women who will run as fast as they can when the bonus is half a million dollars. Mother wants a scion of one of the old families to help me continue the line. Does she care if he is a pig, a drunkard, a wife beater? No, as long as he's from the right family."

"Sounds like she and Pinkney deserve one another."

"Well, she is a little more refined in her approach, but yeah, you could say so. She doesn't care about my feelings, or my happiness, as long as there is an heir to the Balle legacy."

"Wasn't your father the actual member of the Balle family?"

"Yes, he was. My mother married, as they say, above her station, and took on the mantle of defending the family's heritage with a vengeance, like she was trying to prove her worth at being a member of the family."

Amanda thought about that for a moment. "I take it she's done some serious damage to your social life."

Caitlin laughed, but with no humor. "At this point, what social life? Dinner with you is the most 'social life' I've had in the past year. She keeps trying to hook me up with men she thinks are 'suitable.' Unfortunately, at this point, that includes dedicated lushes, or men with a taste for young blondes who they discard before they hit thirty. The last one she tried to get me to date is fourteen years older than me and just got through his third divorce. Even if I could stand the thought of being with a man, I wouldn't be with anyone like that."

"What has she done to the women you've dated?"

"What women there have been have not fared well. My first lover was in my senior year in college. My mother decided that it was just a college experiment and a phase that I would be over as soon as the woman disappeared. She scared the bejesus out of her by threatening her career options. She was studying to be a teacher."

"Damn – does she really have those kind of connections? Not to mention what kind of person tries to destroy the career of a teacher?"

"One who wants to get what she wants and will not stop at anything to get it."

"And the payoff?"

"Oh, that was me being stupid. I was seeing someone while I was working on my master's. I didn't realize she was after me for the family money. My mother figured her for a gold digger and handed her what she wanted."

"I'm not even going to ask what else she's done. All I would do is get really angry."

"How do you think I feel? So for me, it's just easier to do my job and stay single."

"Sounds lonely."

"I have a few friends, I love my work, and I get by. And when she drives me absolutely crazy, well, you heard what happens."

"I honestly don't know what to say to you. I can tell you that I would be happy to continue to enjoy your company while I'm here – no strings and no expectations except pleasant company and damned good food!"

They laughed at that just as the waitress arrived at their table, laid down a large sheet of butcher paper, and dumped a bucket of shrimp, crabs, potatoes, sausage, and corn in the middle of it. Two plates, two sets of shell crackers, and two large cups of melted butter and two of cocktail sauce were added to the table. The waitress looked at them and asked, "More beer?"

Amanda nodded enthusiastically, since she'd already shoved a shrimp into her mouth.

Caitlin just laughed.

After a few quiet minutes of both happily tearing into the pile of food in front of them, Amanda looked at Caitlin rather thoughtfully.

"You know, my folks weren't real thrilled when I told them I was gay. As I said, my mother hoped it was just a phase. For the next couple of years, whenever they had any kind of social event, she made sure that there were at least one or two eligible men available to meet me. It got to the point where I stopped going to my mother's parties except for Thanksgiving and Christmas. That got her to take a different approach—she started inviting eligible women."

Caitlin laughed at that, then got serious again. "I know those feelings. Wish I could avoid Mother's parties, but much of my work is socializing with people who will give money to the museum, so I can't escape!"

ON SATURDAY MORNING, Amanda put on a pair of waders over her canvas britches, threw a pair of hiking boots into the passenger seat of her Jeep, and headed out to the Point. She parked but didn't bother going into the trailer. Instead, she pulled out her notebook, clapped her straw hat on her head, and started walking the shoreline, looking for indications of previous constructions and for hints as to the changes in the shorelines over the years. It was clear to her trained eye that over the years, what had once been a rather wide channel had filled in with sand and debris that gave a grand home for the mangroves that grew on the far side of the creek.

She reached the point where Hobcaw Creek joined with the Wando River. The silt that washed down from the creek had settled into the river. If this was to be used for anything larger than a flat bottom fishing boat, they would have to dredge the whole length of the creek and out into the Wando.

She had started looking for alternatives.

CHAPTER 4

CAITLIN'S PHONE RANG WHILE SHE WAS BALANCED on top of the library ladder trying to retrieve a large, rather dusty document box from the top of the shelves beside the fireplace. She let it keep ringing as she finished pulling the box from the shelf, hugged it to her chest, and carefully climbed down the steps of the ladder. It was on its sixth ring as she sat the box on the desk and tried to dust off her shirt, not very successfully. At the eighth ring, she gave up and picked up the receiver. The only person she knew who would call her at this hour of the morning and then let her phone ring that long was her mother.

"Hello, Mother. How are you this bright Sunday morning?"

"My, my. Have you gotten one of those caller ID things?"

"No, but you are the only person who would call me this early on a Sunday morning and let the phone ring for eight rings before giving up."

"Actually, dear, I thought I might be waking you up, so I let the phone ring."

"No, I've been up since about six this morning. I'm going through all the old records and document boxes looking for the deed to Hobcaw."

"Oh, my, how nasty. Those old boxes probably have more dust than paper at this point."

"Yes, they are dusty – interesting, but I'm something of a mess." Caitlin laughed.

"Well, you will need to get cleaned up this afternoon."

"What now, Mother?"

"Oh, some of the folks with the Huguenot Society are having a tea dance this afternoon. I understand that the attendance will be rather good and I'd like for us to go. Can you be ready by three? I think that green sundress of yours would be lovely. And please wear stockings. I was so embarrassed at the garden party last month when you went bare legged."

Caitlin heaved a heavy sigh. She really needed to find that deed. "Mother, I'd rather not. Those tea dances are really for the over fifty crowd. I usually feel like the kid whose parents couldn't find a sitter." She thought to herself, 'and they're for old school Southern 'aristocrats' who fantasize themselves as part of the British nobility during the Gilded Age.'"

"Well, whether you like it or not, I'll be there at three o'clock. Be wearing the sundress, stockings, and heels." Before Caitlin could make any kind of response, she heard the click of the phone being hung up.

"Damn, damn, DAMN, DAMN!!!!" She stomped in a circle around the library. "Why do I let her do these things to me? WHY!" She shook her head, then took herself to the kitchen to make a cup of tea before she tackled the next box of records.

"At least it will be over by seven, and if I'm lucky I can get her to leave at six." After years of living alone, Caitlin was used to being able to talk to herself without being considered crazy.

AMANDA SPENT Sunday morning going over every aerial picture and plat map for the Hobcaw area and comparing them to her notes from her previous day's slog through the mud flats that made up the shore of most of Hobcaw. As she worked, a small grin slowly made its way to her face. "'Okay, all I need are the sounding results and I may have an answer for Caitlin – and a better solution for the county."

She grinned again, this time over the thought of surprising her new friend. She pulled on her shoes and headed out to a place she'd heard had great sandwiches. The Tattooed Moose was famous (or infamous) for interesting and very tasty bar food. Amanda ordered two duck clubs, made with confit duck, bacon, and cheddar cheese. She added a large order of duck fat fries and a basket of boiled peanuts. Then she headed down to Caitlin's house.

Promptly at noon, she knocked on Caitlin's door, her bag of goodies in one hand and a sheaf of papers in the other.

"What the fuck? She can't be here this early," grumped Caitlin as she unloaded the pile of paper in her lap and walked toward the front door, still covered in dust, scraps of paper, and the occasional bit of spider web.

She yanked the door open, growling, "Mother, you're too early," as she realized it wasn't her mother standing there, but a grinning Amanda.

"Can I come in? I've brought a peace offering for disturbing your Sunday."

"Oh, God. I'm sorry I growled at you. I thought you were my mother!"

"I assumed," smirked Amanda as she eased into the front hall.

"Oh, sorry. Come on into the kitchen. Can I get you something to drink?"

"Sure – after you wash up," Amanda teased gently.

Caitlin laughed, then went to the sink to scrub up. "A shower would be better, but..."

"I'd rather you not retreat to the shower every time I come to see you here." Amanda laughed. "I might get some sort of a complex, thinking you needed to shower as a result of being around me. I promise, I'm not slimy."

Drying her hands and face on a dish towel, Caitlin swatted at Amanda with the slightly damp cloth. "No, you're not slimy, even if your boss is."

"Anyway, I stopped at the Tattooed Moose and brought us some goodies for lunch," said Amanda, quickly changing the subject.

"Ooohh, I love their duck sandwiches."

"Good, 'cause I got us a couple."

"Oh, yum. What other goodies did you bring?"

"Fries and peanuts."

"Boiled peanuts! The way to any good South

Carolinian's heart. Then you must have some limeade to wash it down. Fortunately, I have some in the fridge."

Caitlin pulled a couple of plates out of one cabinet and a couple of glasses out of another. She grabbed a large pitcher out of the ice box, some ice from the freezer, and within a minute had two frosty glasses of limeade. Amanda grabbed the plates and started laying out the sandwiches and fries on them while Caitlin brought the drinks to the table.

The two dug into their lunches. Caitlin didn't realize how hungry she was, and Amanda just watched her revel in the delicious comfit duck sandwich. She was very pleased with herself for finding something that was accepted as a treat.

Once the sandwiches and fries had been consumed, Caitlin looked at the bucket of boiled peanuts with an impish look on her face. "Have you ever had a boiled peanut?"

"No, can't say I have, but I love peanuts roasted in the shell."

"Oh, you are in for a treat. Roasted peanuts are just dry and crunchy. Boiled peanuts melt in your mouth!"

"Okay. I'm game. They looked like something you would like."

"They ARE something I like." Caitlin grinned. "Take one, crack it like you would a roasted peanut, and watch out – the brine can be drippy."

Amanda carefully cracked a peanut open and promptly sprayed herself with very salty brine.

Caitlin chucked. "I warned you."

Amanda extracted the peanut from its shell and carefully tasted the little morsel. The look on her face was priceless – a combination of awe and amazement. The next peanut went in a lot faster.

Between them, the whole bucket of peanuts was gone within fifteen minutes.

Both women had to wash up after that adventure, as they were both lightly coated with peanut brine. As they dried their faces, hands and arms, Caitlin asked, "I take it you found something?"

"Well, it depends on how stubborn an ass Pinkney is going to be, but yes. If you look at Hobcaw Creek, it has silted in pretty seriously over the last century, so the whole thing will have to be dredged to be viable. That's expensive. In addition, most of the shore is a mud flat. That means we will have to build over them to reach the harbor and creek. That's also expensive, both to build and to maintain. There's a way to have the yacht club they want without those expenses – to build it at the end of the point with docking on the Wando River."

"You think you can appeal to their wallets?"

"Well, to the rest of the board. I think Pinkney is obsessed with the little harbor.

"I've got the dredging company coming in tomorrow. I'll have them do an analysis of the depths and then they can give me an estimate of the total dredging cost. I'll have them do an estimate of maintenance dredging as well. Then we'll see what happens."

"Okay. I hope it works. In the meantime, I'll trust my lawyer to slow the process down while I look for the deed and Sarah tries to get it protected as a historic site." Caitlin looked at Amanda, a look of honest gratitude on her face. "I can't thank you enough for what you're trying to do for me.

Somehow, I have to believe one or all of us will prevail." She smiled and placed a gentle kiss on Amanda's cheek. "Now, I hate to do this, but I'm going to have to throw you out. My mother will be here in a while to take me to a tea dance, and I have to get cleaned up and dressed." She paused for a moment, then added, "And no, I REALLY don't want to go, but she sort of trapped me into it."

Amanda stood, smiling at her hostess. "I understand, believe me. I've been trapped before myself. You know, I was thinking, I know you have to go through a pile of papers and records. I could help you next weekend, or maybe some evening this week, if you'd like."

"I'd like that very much. Why don't I call you when I escape from the clutches of my mother's social pretentious?"

"I look forward to it."

Caitlin walked Amanda to the front door. "Thanks again for lunch. It was delicious."

She watched as the engineer left, then turned and trudged upstairs to get ready for her mother.

SAMUEL PACED UP and down the length of the library, muttering under his breath. "Damned Yankee. What is that God-forsaken descendant of the Sherman pig doing in our home? She should be pitched out on her arse."

"Now, husband, do not condemn the child for the acts of the father." Siobhan gently patted her husband's shoulder. "She is trying to help, to preserve our legacy. Accept what she is doing as part of an atonement for what her ancestor did."

"I shall. But I dinna hae to like it."

"And do not begrudge young Caitlin the pleasure of having an honest friend."

"Aye, the lass needs friends, but does it hae to be a damned Sherman?"

"It is who it is. Who can argue what God puts before us, Samuel?"

"Well, I wish young Cat would find the damned deed. I wish I could guide her to the right place to look."

"Well, ye canna. Perhaps..." Siobhan had a suspicion that Amanda might be a help in that matter.

HARRIET BALLE STOOD in Caitlin's entrance hall tapping her foot impatiently. "Could you move a little faster? I would prefer not to be late."

'I would prefer to be anywhere else,' thought the unwilling daughter. "I'll be right down. Let me just check my makeup." 'I hate wearing makeup, especially in this weather. It's almost as bad as stockings.'

"Come on, child. I believe that charming Mr. DuBose will be there today. I know you and he are friends."

"Yes, Mother. And that's all Mr. DuBose and I are – friends." Andrew DuBose had been one of Caitlin's instructors in undergraduate school. He had at least fifteen years on her – not to mention that he was as queer as a three-dollar bill.

They made their way to Harriet's car and silently got in. While the location of the tea dance was only three blocks away in the garden at Mrs. Whaley's Garden Museum,

Harriet Balle did NOT walk – ever, even when it took longer to park than it took to drive there.

The two women walked into the Whaley House. Like Caitlin's, it was originally a pre-revolutionary home that had been modified over the years until it was made into a museum reminiscent of the 1920s in its furnishings. All of the rooms at the back of the house opened onto a lovely garden that now, at the height of summer, was in full and glorious bloom.

A pianist was playing in one corner of the main reception room, obviously sweating in his tuxedo. It was definitely too hot for a black suit. A long table on the other side of the room held finger foods and non-alcoholic drinks that had evidently not been touched. On the other hand, the bar at the back of the room was doing business hand over fist.

Harriet got a martini while Caitlin settled for a tonic with a slice of lime. She had long ago learned that staying sober when her mother was in matchmaker mode was a very good idea.

Over the course of the next hour, Caitlin politely chatted with a random collection of Charleston's old families' representatives, primarily (politely) 40+ year old women who were friends of her mother's, and a few 50+ gentlemen whose wives had dragged them to this event.

Unexpectedly, Caitlin felt a tap on her shoulder. She turned around and grinned. Andrew DuBose stood there, a questioning look on his face. "Hi, Cat. Long time no see. Your mother still trying to marry you off to a proper Charleston family?"

"Of course she is. Shall we dance? I'd rather she not hear

this conversation. She'd either make a scene or not talk to me for the next month."

"Having her not talk to you for a month could be a blessing, girl."

"Oh, she's my mother. I'm sure she would find any number of ways to make my life miserable."

The two walked out to the dance floor laid out in the garden. The pianist was playing a slow waltz – perfect music to make the motions of dancing while chatting.

"So, she's no closer to accepting you for who you are than she was when you were in college?"

"Not even close. If anything, her blinders have gotten more complete. When I was in college, she could call it a 'phase.' Now it's just my family obligation to keep the Balle line going."

"Well, there are a number of ways you could do that without having to get married to one of us ol' goats."

"Funny you should say that. A friend of mine pointed that out the other day, but I don't want to be a single parent."

"Who says you have to be a single parent? Spencer Rowe and his partner are doing a fine job with their boy."

"How is Spencer's boy doing? I knew they'd adopted an older child, but haven't seen them socially for quite a while. " Caitlin spoke quietly.

"You don't know what's going on because you don't hang out at any of the gay bars, or participate in any of the rainbow events." Andrew swirled them around another couple. "Honey, you need to get out."

"I get out!"

"Yeah, for work or with your mother. Let's try something else."

"Well, I have been seeing the engineer they have looking over the Hobcaw site. She's a charming, witty woman."

"You mean Ms. Sherman? I bet the fact that you're seeing a Sherman is going over with your mother like a lead balloon."

In a rather quiet voice, Caitlin said, "She doesn't know and I would prefer it stay that way."

"This is Charleston. You know she'll hear sooner or later."

"Well, we are just friends, and she's involved with the Hobcaw mess."

"I'm sure Spencer will be able to do something about that."

"I hope so, Andy. I really hope so."

CAITLIN MANAGED to escape from the tea dance or garden party or whatever it was by six o'clock, after the handful of quasi-eligible males had left. She walked home, leaving her lightly inebriated mother gossiping with several of her old friends.

Within ten minutes, she climbed the steps to her front door and walked in, kicking off her high heels as she crossed the threshold. She ran up the stairs to her bedroom, eager to strip off the stockings as soon as possible. The dress, while comfortable, was not as cool as a tank top and a pair of shorts, both of which were on in a matter of minutes.

She glanced through the window into her backyard,

having seen a little movement out of the corner of her eye. Thinking it was the neighbor's cat, she looked out the window and was stunned to see Amanda sitting there sipping on a soda from the local 7-11.

She ran down the stairs and into her back garden. "What the hell are you doing here?"

"Waiting for you. I had something I wanted to ask you about."

"You could have called this evening or at work tomorrow."

"I could have, but then it would have been moot."

"Moot?" Caitlin was bewildered.

"Yup. Moot. Dinner tonight would already be over. Want to go find some seafood – would snot on a shell be good?"

Caitlin laughed. "Let me find some shoes."

"Good. You have led me down a path of sin."

"It's not the best time of the year for oysters. How about some crabs?"

"Oh? I thought the ones we had the other day were delicious."

"Yes, but small. Summer is the breeding season, so we don't get the big ones till September and then through the winter. On the other hand, we've got blue crabs now."

"I'll take what I can get!" Amanda looked a little shy as she said, "And I enjoy the company even more than the food."

Caitlin looked startled, though not displeased. Softly, she replied, "I enjoy the company too."

Their evening was quietly pleasant. They ate, talked, drank a little, laughed, and ate some more. The problem they both faced, one way or another, faded into the background.

THE MOON WAS high when Samuel returned to the Point and took up his seat on the stone, with Siobhan hovering behind him, trying to calm his simmering anger.

"Fae, assemble," he bellowed.

Ciara floated down from the oak, leaning against its solid trunk. Tiernan walked around the trunk, holding his jug in his hand. He offered it to Samuel, who shook his head in annoyance. Quinn stepped in beside him and accepted a draught from him, though.

Samuel looked around. "Where is Birch?"

"Here, Laird."

"Go fetch Ronan for me, lad."

"Aye," he said, running swiftly toward the water.

Kade and Grear were standing politely beside Siobhan, waiting to see what the old Laird wanted from them all.

Soon enough, the Ghillie Dhu and the Selkie came trotting up to stand in front of the Laird, with the Selkie holding his skin over one arm and still dripping water.

"You called, sir?" The selkie's attitude was laconic. Samuel was not the Laird of this mighty sea creature.

Samuel cleared his throat. "Tomorrow, men are coming to start sounding the harbor, and eventually to start dredging. That Sherman woman is going to start testing the mud flats for the parts of the ship yard that are under them to figure out how to cover them so people can walk on them safely. They are going to destroy all that is left of what I and my sons built AND I WILL NOT HAVE IT."

Siobhan put her hand on Samuel's shoulder. "Gently, husband. Gently. Our granddaughter and that Sherman woman are trying to fight the politician to make this a historical site and preserve all that we built."

"Woman, take your hand from me. I will have those interlopers stopped – any way you can, short of causing death." He turned to the Fae standing around him. "Slow them down, stop them, do what you can and what you must, short of death. Am I understood?"

There was a chorus of "Yes, Laird." And one voice that said, "Aye, Samuel."

RONAN STOOD at the edge of Hobcaw Creek looking up and down the waterway, and then turned to look into the little harbor. A slow smile graced his handsome face as he flung the fur he carried around his shoulders. As he dove into the water, he transformed into a sleek gray seal. In a language known only to the creatures of the sea, he called to these western animals, so like and yet so different from the creatures of his youth. He made a simple request—load as much sand and jetsam into the canal as possible. He then set off to collect detritus from various ship wrecks that littered the South Carolina coast.

Meanwhile, Birch took a small forest of weeping willow sprouts and planted them lovingly along the recently dug water and sewer lines. With the appeal of running fresh water so near, they would grow rapidly, their roots seeking out every joint in the newly laid pipes and insinuating themselves through what would become cracks to savor the sweet water.

CAITLIN WALKED to her office that Monday morning feeling pretty good considering the stress in her life.

She found Sarah waiting for her with a thick folder of papers. "Morning, sunshine. I have a task for you. See this pile of paper? You get to fill it out so I can petition for Hobcaw Point to be declared a state historical site."

Caitlin eyed the roughly inch-tall pile of papers. "Um, okay. How long do you think it will take?"

"Oh, it usually takes four to six months once they have all the paperwork, but I think I can expedite the process."

"No, I mean how long will it take to fill it all out?"

Sarah looked at her, wide eyed, for a moment, then broke into deep guffaws. When she could finally talk again, she admitted, "I have no idea. I've never had to do it."

"If I get bogged down, can I come to you for help?"

"As much as I can. As I said, I've never had to do it myself."

Caitlin randomly riffled through the papers for a couple of minutes.

Sarah decided to interrupt her before she got too distracted. "So, how's the search for the deed going?"

"It's a massively slow slog, to be honest. I've found some fascinating information, and once this mess with Pinkney is over, I foresee at least a couple of articles for the academic journals coming forth. But I haven't found the deed. I did find something interesting, though – a sketch of the facilities at the shipyard around 1774 – just before the Revolution. Just based on that sketch alone, I think there's a paper."

"There's more than a paper – there's justification for claiming it as a historical site if the surveyor findings even partially match it. I'd love to see it."

"Of course. I'll call Amanda and see when the plat maps are going to be ready. Perhaps all three of us should get together."

"Excellent – a real family reunion. I look forward to it. Perhaps I'll bring my companion. I think you will like her."

Caitlin stared after the departing woman. Did everyone know about her sexuality? Damn, Sarah was gay. 'I didn't know. I need to get myself a working gaydar,' Caitlin thought.

AMANDA ARRIVED at the trailer at a little before nine o'clock, this time with a thermos of decent coffee prepared the way she liked it with a little sugar and a lot of cream. Until she had time to go to a store and get a coffee maker for the office, it was a necessity.

She heard the putter of a small boat engine, and pulling on her waders so she could cross the mud flat without getting her pants wet, she wandered out to meet the dredging company's sounding crew. "Good morning," she hailed as they nudged up to the bank.

"Miss Sherman?"

"Yes, that's me."

"So, how far are we going to go, ma'am?"

"I need soundings all across this little harbor, then out into the creek and down to the main channel in the Wando River, please. How long do you think it will take?"

"If we don't finish it today, and I suspect we won't, we will have it done sometime tomorrow morning, ma'am."

"Excellent. I should be in the office or on the property until about four this afternoon, so if you need me, don't hesitate to come and ask."

"Yes, ma'am. Have a good day."

Amanda trooped back to the trailer, listening to the putt-putt of the sounding boat as it crisscrossed the little harbor. Soon it mixed with the sounds of the groundsmen as they valiantly continued to fight against the weeds, vines, saw grass, and sandspurs that covered much of the property.

She had a bunch of drawings to create so she could start estimating the effort needed to create the infrastructure for a decent yacht club. The architects who were designing the buildings would need her drawings so they could understand where they could place the buildings for the facility and what kind of foundations would be needed.

Shortly after ten that morning, Amanda heard a car pull up outside. Putting down her drawing tools and dropping her glasses on the drawing table, she went to the door to see who her visitors were.

"Good morning, Miss Sherman. We have your maps completed." The man who hailed her lifted a rather large document tube. "I brought your copy over, while my boss took the originals to Mr. Pinkney. Do you want to look them over?"

"Sure. Come on in and we'll see what's there."

CHAPTER 5

AMANDA SPENT THE NEXT THREE DAYS WORKING over a massively complex map of the entire Hobcaw Point site – from the curve of the creek that signaled the beginning of the property to the main channel in the Wando River that bordered the western edge of the property. She had spent part of Tuesday morning outside with a long prod, looking for signs of the old shipyard buried under the mud flats.

She had stopped by Caitlin's on Monday evening and collected a copy of the 1774 sketch of the site. She overlayed that information on the plat map that the surveyor had provided, sketching in the original buildings, which for the most part confirmed what the surveyors had found plus what she'd detected under the mud. She also layered in the sounding results, showing how heavily silted both the harbor and the creek had become over time. She also showed how using the side of the point that faced on the Wando River would be far more efficient, both in terms of cost and access for the users.

She also put together a table of comparative advantages of the Wando Shore and the Hobcaw Harbor.

The final data points she assembled was a comparison of the relative costs of building and maintaining the two sites.

On Friday morning, she was ready to face the board with her weekly engineering report. She anticipated rather mixed results.

She dressed very carefully, wanting to look as professional and polished as possible, though it didn't help that the day was gray, and it was raining in sheets. It was always so difficult to look very finished and put together when everything was slightly damp, no matter how hard she tried. She even wore a skirt, blouse, and jacket as well as the hated stockings and heels, instead of her usual slacks and dress boots. A little makeup, a knee-length rain coat, and an umbrella finished her ensemble.

Taking her laptop so she could project her drawings and tables, as well as the original and overlayed drawings in the large tube, she faced the door of the county administration building, took a deep breath, and entered what she had grown to think of as the lion's den. And she knew she was no Daniel.

She entered the board room and hooked her computer up to the projector. She carefully pinned her drawings to the display wall on one side of the room. Then she collected a cup of moderately decent coffee and waited for the board members to arrive.

One by one, they drifted in, some making a bee line to the coffee pot, others wandering over to peruse the posted drawings with interest. The last to arrive was Pinkney, who swaggered in as he expected a report that would allow the real work to start on his pet project.

Amanda stayed at the back of the room while Pinkney, as chairman, dispatched some ordinary business with the council. He then invited Amanda to present her findings.

"Ladies and gentlemen, I have had an opportunity to evaluate the options and challenges presented to the construction of a yacht club on the property know as Hobcaw Point." She put up the aerial view of the property from the central channel of the Wando River to the defining curve of Hobcaw Creek.

"We have had the entire area surveyed, from the border on the Wando River, around the point, and back to the curve of Hobcaw Creek where the little delta begins, and that defines the eastern edge of the property. The survey also tracked against Hobcaw Drive and North Hobcaw Drive. The gray areas in the aerial photograph are mud flats, which, as you can see, define much of the shore of Hobcaw Creek."

She projected the first overlay, with the aerial photograph faded to gray behind it so that the real image could be seen beneath the plat drawing. "This image reflects the findings of the surveying team. As you can see, there are a few docks that residents of Hobcaw Drive have imposed to allow access to the creek. They are unauthorized by the owner of the Hobcaw Point property. As you can also see, there are a number of foundations remaining from the original buildings that were damaged at the end of the Civil War. We have identified the main house, a blacksmith's shop, a carpenter's shop, what we think was a rope walk, and a number of other smaller outbuildings." As she named off each building, she pointed out the ruins of each.

Her next overlay showed the findings they had made in the mud flats. "For a variety of reasons that will come clear shortly, we believe that the mud flats are fairly recent additions to the shore line. Using metal probes, we have sampled parts of the flats to determine if there are any additional foundations or constructions that have been buried by the mud. In doing so, we have found what we think was probably a dry dock under the mud flat to the east of the harbor. We have also determined that the harbor itself was once considerably larger than it is today, as we think we've found the remains of at least one pier under the flat to the west of the harbor."

"Based on our analysis, we also believe that at one point, the creek was considerably wider than it is today, offering much clearer access to the Wando River."

"In addition to having the land surveyed in detail, we have also had the waterway sounded to determine the depth of the harbor and creek, and thus determine what dredging would need to be done to first make a viable harbor for recreational boats – both motorized and sail boats, and a projection of what would need to be done to maintain the facility over time." With that, she overlaid the depth mapping of the waterways.

"To further substantiate our findings, we have acquired a drawing of the site that was created in the mid-1700s which shows that our findings correspond rather closely to the drawing of the original site." She overlaid the sketch that Caitlin had provided. "The Charleston Museum was kind enough to provide this information as confirmation of our findings. They have been evaluating the site as a possible historical site for Charleston County and have begun the process to have it declared as such." Amanda paused to let the implications of that statement soak in.

"As a final challenge to the development of a yacht club at the little harbor, there is an old cemetery on the property. To construct the proposed yacht club, we would have to obtain the permission of the family to move the cemetery, which is a rather complex challenge."

There were several groans around the table. They were all perfectly well aware of Caitlin Balle's challenge to their plans.

Amanda let them all groan and gripe about the challenges and the costs. She then cleared her throat loudly to get their attention. "There is an alternative that you may wish to consider. As you can see, the land at the mouth of the creek and bordering on the river is clear, has no remnants of an earlier construction, does not require extensive dredging, and is still part of the area known as Hobcaw Point."

As Amanda talked, Pinkney was getting more and more frustrated. His dream was to have the yacht club named after him and be established on the historic site, not sitting on the river. He knew that the museum people had been looking at the site, and had planned to circumvent their curiosity by acting with speed, knowing how slowly the Historical Commission acted when considering creating a historical site. He stood abruptly from his seat at the table. "Miss Sherman, you will continue to prepare the original site for construction of a yacht club. We planned and budgeted for this site, not for a site along the river, and that's what we are paying you to do. So do it." With that, he stalked out of the conference room.

Amanda just stood there, staring at the abruptly slammed door for a moment. She took a deep breath and looked around at the other county commissioners.

One older man looked up at her and politely asked, "Miss Sherman, do you have any more information for us to consider?"

"Well, I have done a comparison of the challenges and advantages of each site. I have also done an estimate of the costs of dealing with the challenges." She pulled up the challenges and advantages table up on the screen, and the conversation with the other commissioners continued, with her concluding with the cost savings of placing the yacht club on the bank of the Wando River.

"So, you're saying that the old natural harbor presents a lot of challenges and will be expensive to build and maintain when we could build at the junction of the Waldo and Hobcaw for a lot less money and a lot fewer problems?"

"Yes, sir."

"But the current contract says to build at the old harbor and our fearless leader says to keep doing what you were hired to do?"

"Obviously, sir. You heard him."

The commissioner patted Amanda on the shoulder. "Miss Sherman, keep doing what you're doing. Support the museum people. And look very closely at the Wando River site, so when we move the yacht club there, you'll be ready."

"Yes, sir. Thank you, sir."

When Amanda left the building, the temperature had risen to the mid-nineties, and it was still raining. At this rate, the work site would be solid mud on Monday. She headed for home, more than ready to shed her now damp and decidedly uncomfortable stocking, heels, and suit. She needed a shower.

CAITLIN LEFT work early that afternoon. She decided that the evening with Amanda, Sarah and her partner deserved something better than pizza, so she headed home to put together a decent, but relaxed dinner.

The night before, she'd made a nice cold cucumber soup. It was creamy, and for weather like they were having, very cooling and refreshing. She had taken a few minutes that morning to boil up a couple of pounds of shrimp, which she was going to reduce to shrimp salad in a remoulade sauce when she got home. She had the makings for a nice pot of pimento cheese, some cold cuts and cheeses, carrots, celery, and radishes, crackers, and a baguette. A bowl of fresh strawberries with sour cream, brown sugar and honey for dipping completed a lovely summer supper.

WHEN AMANDA LEFT HER APARTMENT, blessedly showered and changed into shorts, trainers and a short-sleeved cotton shirt, a light mist was falling. By the time she was two blocks away, the sky opened up and rain came down in sheets. Within seconds, the road was covered with water running swiftly, overflowing the gutters, and making driving difficult. She slowed her Jeep and continued toward Caitlin's. It was more like boating than driving.

Sarah and Savannah had arrived at Caitlin's just before

the deluge broke. Laughing, they dashed from their car to the porch, with just a few drops dampening their shoulders, but before they could rap on the door knocker, the rain hit with a vengeance. It came down so hard and so quickly that their shoes were soaked by the backsplash off the steps.

Amanda pulled into the driveway just a few minutes later and headed for the kitchen door. In the less than ten feet she had to travel to reach that entrance, she was soaked. Fortunately, the document tube she carried was plastic and kept her precious drawings dry. Her computer case was also waterproof. The rest of her, unfortunately, was not.

She burst into Caitlin's kitchen without knocking, then stood in the doorway, dripping.

The three other women looked at her, expressions ranging from startled to surprised to sympathetic painted on their faces.

Caitlin was the first to respond. "Here, give me your things, shed the shoes, and we'll do something to get you dry."

Amanda handed her computer case and document carrier to Sarah, leaned over to untie her shoes and stripped them off, along with her socks. By then, Caitlin had found a kitchen towel that she used to dry her face and ruffle the worst of the water out of her hair.

Caitlin just looked at Amanda, shaking her head. "Come with me. I think I can find something that will fit you, since we're about the same size." She turned to Sarah and Savannah. "Make yourselves at home. Anything in the fridge is fair game. And could you put the kettle on? I think our little swamp fox here could probably use a cup of tea when we get her dried off."

Amanda looked at the other guests and with a rather shy grin, ducked her head in greeting and dutifully followed Caitlin upstairs.

Caitlin led the way to the master bedroom and directly into the attached bath. It wasn't huge, but it was well appointed, with an old-fashioned claw foot tub and a fairly modern separate shower, a nice sink and counter that held an assortment of lotions, hair products, a brush and comb, and a toothbrush holder and tooth paste. Amanda noticed that there was only one toothbrush. A modern low-flow toilet had been installed. But right now, the best thing in the room was a large cabinet that held, among other things, several large, fluffy towels.

"Get yourself stripped and dry," commanded Caitlin as she tossed a towel to Amanda, "While I go find you some shorts and a shirt. I think you'll need some underwear too."

Amanda blushed, but agreed. "Yes, well, I'm pretty much wet all the way through."

"I don't think I have a bra that will fit you since you're bigger in the shoulders and chest than I am, but I'm sure my panties will work. As for shorts – a size 10? And a medium t-shirt?"

Amanda's blush deepened. "Um, yes, although a size large t-shirt would be more comfortable."

"Let me see what I can find." Caitlin chuckled.

Left alone for a couple of minutes, Amanda stripped out of her soggy clothing, toweled off, and wrapped the towel around herself, waiting for Caitlin and dry clothing, and grateful that her hostess used bath sheets large enough to offer her some marginal sense of modesty.

"Here you go." Caitlin froze for a moment, regarding the

ivory skin of Amanda's' shoulders and the top of her breast, which were a sharp contrast with her deeply tanned arms and face. The woman's legs were elegantly muscled, not too heavily, but beautifully defined, and ending in slender ankles and feet. Again, the tan lines were distinctive, with smooth ivory skin on her feet and upper thighs sandwiching deeply tanned legs. Her profession was defined by her tan lines.

Caitlin fumbled for a moment, then set the clothes down on the counter. "When you're dressed, come on downstairs. You want Earl Gray, Irish Breakfast or hibiscus tea?"

"Irish Breakfast with a splash of milk, please."

DINNER for the four women was a pleasant way to pass some time. Caitlin's cooking was well appreciated, and the sweet white wine she served with it was just the right lubricant for the four of them to shed any hesitancy and tell amusing tales on themselves. As Sarah and Savannah were both about twenty years older than Caitlin and Amanda, they devolved into providing advise on how to successfully keep their lives private and live relatively normal and fulfilling lives as lesbians in the socially driven Charleston society.

"The term is 'companions.' That way, there's no sexual implication while everyone knows that you're off the market and they leave you alone. Hell, our parents treat us the same way they treat our married siblings and their partners."

Savannah, who was an architect, added, "In fact, I think that 'companions' has been an accepted relationship within

Charleston society for a long time. My aunt lived with her companion for over forty years and no one seemed to have a problem with it. Most of my clients ask after Sarah every time they see me, just as they ask after the wives of the men in my office, so all you have to do is keep your head down and use the right terminology." She laughed at her own pragmatism.

"But how do you meet someone?" Caitlin asked.

Sarah laughed. "Look around you, dear. Family is everywhere. You just have to look."

Caitlin and Amanda glanced at one another, a look of recognition on one face and of appreciation on the other.

SAMUEL AND SIOBHAN were leaning against the buffet in the dining room, listening to this little exchange. Samuel glowered. "I told you I dinna like that damned Yankee courting our girl."

"Husband, if there is love, it canna be all bad, and none of the men that have been through have been ... acceptable. You know that the philanderer, or the alcoholic, or the wastrel that her mother has dragged into her life have been atrocious. What if this woman is decent and makes her happy?"

"She canna give her children. We need her to have an heir. By all that is holy, wife, she's a God-Be-Damned SHERMAN!"

"She is not the damned general. Let us see what she does before we condemn her to the lowest circle of hell." Siobhan popped out of the house and back to her stone to sit and brood over her granddaughter's predicament and her husband's bull-headedness.

~

AFTER THE STRAWBERRIES were consumed and the coffee was brewing, Sarah turned to Amanda with a questioning look in her eyes. "So, oh clever engineer, what have you gone and found for us?"

"Well, I think you'll be quite happy with what I've got. Let me show you." She pulled her document tube out and opened it. "Here you have the current plat map of the area with actual boundaries of the Hobcaw Point property marked out. We've also mapped all of the building foundations that are on the property and the cemetery. In the areas that are now mud flats, we've done some soundings using steel probes. Where you see these red dots, we've found rock, concrete, or wood under the mud at a depth of about eighteen inches. While we have not excavated to determine the exact nature of these findings, we have reason to believe that there are additional foundations under the mud."

She pulled another drawing out and laid it over the plat map. "Here is the sketch that Caitlin found that laid out the plan for the site from the 18th century. When I overlayed the sketch and the current site map, the match is very close. And here, where it shows the dry dock on the drawings, our probes found evidence of structures under the mud. We also found evidence of this dock shown on the old drawing."

Sarah grinned, excited at the things Amanda had found. "I think this will give us the ammo we need to have Hobcaw declared a historic site. This is excellent!"

Amanda smiled ruefully. "Well, that's the good news. I also pointed out to the commissioners that they would be in a much better position if they put their yacht club over at the junction of the creek and the Wando – it would be cheaper to build, they wouldn't be running over old foundations, they wouldn't have to move an old cemetery even if Caitlin agreed, and they wouldn't have to dredge hundreds of tons of mud out of the harbor and creek."

"All good, sound logic," Savannah commented. "It makes good financial sense."

"It may make good financial sense, but don't bother to tell Pinkney that. He has his heart set on putting it on the site of the old shipyard. He's ordered me to continue with making the site ready for construction."

Caitlin blew through her teeth. "I'll call Spencer tomorrow and ask him to step up the heat. Unless and until I find that damned deed, that's the best I can do."

Sarah drummed her fingers on the table. "Bring these drawings to the office on Monday and we'll go to the Historical Commission and see if we can rush it through."

Savannah looked thoughtful. "I wonder if getting one of the local politicians involved would do any good? Not the county guys, but someone higher up in the chain of command."

Sarah looked at her, frowning a little. "I don't think it could hurt. I wish we could get the press involved. Pinkney doesn't respond well to rational thought, but I suspect the little weasel doesn't like being the object of ridicule in the press."

Caitlin grinned. "I think that can be arranged. My college roommate is a reporter for the Post and Courier."

"Excellent!" Sarah was definitely excited.

A little hesitantly, Amanda spoke up. "Could you, um, keep me out of the paper, please? I really do need this job however it works out."

RONAN STUCK his head up out of the water, looking at the odd foot-long fish who was patiently waiting for the big seal's attention. The mudskipper was perched on its downward angled fins, waiting at the edge of the mud flats. "Lord Ronan, in the past two tides, my kith and kin have burrowed through the mud, leaving a maze of tunnels that would sink any human who happened to step on top of them up to their hips. What else would you have us do, my lord?"

"Would to set the same kind of tunnels along the shore line, my fish brother?"

"Yes, my lord. It shall be done."

Ronan smiled a seal grin, a terrifying look for any fish that was potential dinner for the pinniped.

Ronan swam over to the tangle of saw grass, calling for the leader of the snapping turtle colony that resided in the roots. His instructions to the taciturn, and frankly anti-social animal were simple. "Bite any human who comes near you and yours."

A grunt was all the acknowledgement he received. It was enough.

Ronan spent the rest of the night artfully spreading bits of jetsam, remnants of various ship wrecks along the outer islands, designed to complicate the process of dredging the waterways.

While Ronan was creating havoc under the water and at the coast line, Birch was busily encouraging his plant friends to make things more difficult. He visited his rapidly growing weeping willows, encouraging them to creep into the water pipes and savor the sweet water. He encouraged the salt hay and cane to spread their tangled roots in the soft mire just above the mud flats, making access more difficult. All over the property, various shrubs burst into bloom, spreading their branches – and their roots – to establish a dense undergrowth that ensured slow, miserable labor to clear. Button bush, titi, yaupon holly with its spiky leaves, swamp rose with its long, vicious spikes, and saw palmetto with sharp, tough leaves and spiked edges seemed to grow overnight. In fact, it did grow overnight, responding to Birch's gentle songs.

With the burst of growth came another plague. A plague of bugs. The combination of puddles of stagnant water from the rain, and the presence of humans with nice, warm, protein filled blood set every female mosquito into breeding mode, which made more mosquitoes that needed to breed. By the Monday following the Friday downpour, the mosquitoes would be so thick they would appear to be black clouds swarming across the site.

There was another aspect to the explosion in the mosquito population. The largest roach in the Americas – the palmetto bug – spread its wings and joyously flew into the clouds of mosquitos, consuming them in mass. This resulted in the three-inch insect monsters maniacally breeding. But their diet wasn't limited to other bugs. They ate pretty much anything – insulation on wires, glue, gloves, boots, cotton, left overs – anything. The only things immune to these six-legged, winged eating machines were plastics and metals.

Tiernan called a small, furry friend of his – a little black and white masked fellow with as much of a sense of humor as he had. Together, Bandito and Tiernan found a way into the trailer. From that point on, nothing was safe.

Grear, Kade, and Quinn conferred and concluded that they could do small annoying things until heavier equipment arrived. In the meantime, they emptied gas cans, stripped wires, carefully "lost" any document that was left out and looked important, and generally made nuisances of themselves.

By the time Amanda and the crew returned to Hobcaw Point on Monday, the place was a god-forsaken mess. It was bad enough that Amanda called the police to report vandalism.

When the cops arrived, they looked around at the mess, then looked around outside. They found some very clear foot prints—raccoon foot prints. All around the trailer, inside the trailer, and in the area where the crew kept the garbage cans.

The cops laughed, and one of them said, "Be sure to lock your doors and windows, lady." They left.

Amanda stood there, watching them leave and fuming. She then carefully looked around the trailer herself. Under the raccoon prints she found the remainders of a small man's or a boy's boot print. It was not like any boot worn by her crew nor was it like her boots. Hell, her foot was larger than that print.

Amanda stewed as she cleaned up the mess in the trailer. Her crew boss had similar problems out in the tools shed to deal with. It was not a good morning for anyone – except the two small brown figures hidden in a corner snickering to one another.

CAITLIN AND SARAH spent Monday morning going through the documentation to request Hobcaw be declared a historic site, adding the information that Amanda had provided the night before. At lunch, they were joined by Caitlin's college roommate, Beth Dauntry. By the end of the meal, Beth was planning a whole series of articles, providing the historical perspective, the political perspective, the budgetary questions, and the damage the planned yacht club would do to Mount Pleasant's greatest historical site. Pinkney was screwed, or at least they hoped he was. It would depend on whether Beth's editor would print the proposed series.

Caitlin walked home that evening feeling very positive and hopeful. Yes, she still had to find the original deed, but with all of these other factors in play, she hoped that her family's legacy would at least be preserved, even if it was in the ownership of the county.

She had just slipped off her shoes and wandered into the kitchen to pour herself a glass of iced tea and contemplate the contents of the fridge for dinner. An unexpected and very loud banging on her front door drew her out of her pleasant contemplation.

"Who the hell is hammering on my door?" she mumbled

as she slowly walked through the front hall. She peaked out of the window beside the door and saw a very disheveled and obviously angry Amanda standing there.

She flung the door open and cried, "Amanda! What's wrong?"

Amanda stomped into the hall. "What's wrong? WHAT'S WRONG? You know perfectly well what's wrong. I thought we were friends. I thought you trusted me to help protect your god damned legacy of old foundations, ancient tombstones, and flipping mud. So why did you have the site vandalized? What overwhelming brilliant idea did you have when you turned that raccoon loose in my office!" With each sentence, Amanda's voice rose until she was bellowing at Caitlin.

Caitlin backed up a couple of steps from this raging woman, waiting until she blew out. She had learned the wisdom of treating a temper tantrum like you did a hurricane – let it blow out and then go about repairing the damage.

Once Amanda had wound down and stood there simply panting, her anger still radiating from her, Caitlin began trying to figure out what had happened.

"Okay. For starters, whatever you think I did, I was here last night. After you left, I cleaned the kitchen, took a shower, and went to bed. Why don't you tell me what happened?"

Amanda was still breathing heavily, so Caitlin took her hand and pulled her into the kitchen, pushed her into a chair at the table, and then pulled two glasses out of the cabinet and poured them both some iced tea.

"Okay. So start talking. And skip the yelling."

Amanda explained all the things that had happened out at the site. "I swear, someone is trying to sabotage this project. I don't know anyone other than you who has a motive to do that, so I assumed..."

"Well, I'm many things, but I'm not a saboteur." Caitlin sat for a few minutes, tapping her chin with her index finger. "All I can think of would probably make you think I'm crazy."

"Well, since I'm already going crazy, try me."

"The founders of our family came to South Carolina after the Jacobite Rebellion failed. Samuel Balle was Scottish, and his wife Siobhan was Irish. They settled here, and eventually built the first phase of the shipyard at Hobcaw. The family built or repaired trading vessels that supported the Carolina cotton and rice trades. They also supported the fishing community. During the Revolution, they built small, fast craft that were successful blockade runners. The shipyard continued to grow, and during the Civil War they built ships for the Confederacy, again specializing in fast blockade runners. In 1865, General Sherman had the whole facility burned to the ground because of the damage that ships built here had done during the war. My family diversified and recovered from the impact of the war within a generation or two. We stayed in the Charleston area, but never went back into ship building."

Amanda nodded, understanding all of this brief history. She waited for whatever else Caitlin had to say. Clearly, the woman was hesitant to go into the next aspect of her family.

After a long silence and then a deep drink of tea, Caitlin continued. "Rumor has it that Hobcaw Point is haunted – and not just by ghosts. We have a banshee who wails when a member of the family is about to die. She was last heard when my father died. There are those who say that a gray seal lives around the area, but we are way too far south for a gray seal. Legend says there are shape shifting creatures in the Orkneys called Selkies who can either be seen as gray seals or as very handsome men. There have been reports over the years of a dark boy who lives in the woods around the point. The reports of sightings are too many years apart to be the same boy. Yet, the descriptions of him never differ. The family also holds that the spirits of Grandpa Samuel and Grandma Siobhan have remained, guarding their beloved land."

Amanda just sat there, a look of interest on her face and giving no sign of ridicule or disbelief.

Caitlin took a deep breath and continued. "If Grandpa Samuel figured out what Pinkney is trying to do, he would be exceptionally angry. These are the kind of things that Scottish and Irish tradition says are typical of the works of the Fae – elves, fairies, clurichaun, leprechaun, brownies. They're malicious, annoying, destructive, but not malevolent. The only one of the creatures reported who could be actively dangerous or life threatening is the selkie. And a ghost or two could put a serious spanner in the works – literally."

Amanda sat there thinking for a long time. Finally, she sighed. "You know, one of my favorite authors once summed up our situation. He said, 'When you have eliminated all which is impossible, then whatever remains, however improbable, must be the truth.'"

"Who said that?"

"Arthur Conan Doyle had Sherlock Holmes say it. It seems to apply here."

Caitlin sat quietly. Amanda got them more tea.

"Do you think Grandpa Samuel may have hidden the deed?"

"If not outright hidden, perhaps put it someplace safe."

"Do you think he'd help you find it if you asked real nice?"

"All I can do is try."

"Okay. How bout we go find some dinner? I'm starving."

"Let me get my shoes."

CHAPTER 6

Tiernan paced up and down in front of Samuel's tombstone, rubbing his hands and chuckling with glee. Samuel strolled up to his old friend the clurichaun and asked, "So what has you so happy, ol' man?"

"Oh, my little masked friend made an absolute pig wallow of that woman's office. It was beautiful!"

Kade piped up from beside Siobhan's tombstone. "She went stomping out of here cursing Mistress Caitlin's name too."

"Good!" Samuel smiled for the first time in many days. "Mayhap this will convince that bloody Sherman to cease courting my granddaughter."

Siobhan shook her head. In a very soft voice, she said, "Maybe it will convince her that you are sticking your nose in where it dinna belong."

Quinn grinned, having created almost as much of a mess as his cousin in the workmen's tool shed.

Samuel turned to the leprechaun. "What news from you, sir?"

"Ah, a collection of frustrated, angry, and unproductive workers today, Laird."

"May we keep them unproductive, my friend."

Birch slid out from behind a tree. "Um, Ronan asked me to tell you the waterways are ready for what may hap, sir."

"Let me check on the granddaughter, then we shall celebrate our progress." Samuel disappeared. He reappeared in the corner of the kitchen and heard the last few words of the conversation between Caitlin and Amanda. As he returned to his headstone, he was cursing. "What will it take to separate those two? Why must she associate with a damned Yankee – and a bloody Sherman, to boot?"

"Husband, take a deep breath. Poor Caitlin has been lonely for a long time. The atrocious reprobates that her mother keeps pushing at her, and the more appalling acts that woman has taken to keep her away from decent women, have made her life an emotional wasteland. What Stephen was thinking when he wed that horrible social climber Harriet is beyond my imagination."

Ciara broke in, "I will not wail for her when death knocks. She is no true Balle!"

"Whether Harriet is or not a Balle, poor Caitlin is sadly alone. This Amanda, regardless of her ancestry, seems a good person. She is trying to protect Caitlin's heritage, and Caitlin enjoys her company. So donna dare curse at the child. She is doing good, for Hobcaw and for Caitlin. So cease your raving malice, husband. She is not the one who burned the place down."

DINNER WAS A LOW-KEY AFFAIR. Caitlin had driven over to Mount Pleasant to a small, rather run-down looking place on Shem Creek that clearly catered to the local residents, boaters and fishermen, based on the number of boats docked behind the building. On the other hand, the food was fabulous. Caitlin had a bowl of hoppin' john, while Amanda shoveled in a rich Brunswick stew, both happy to have the sturdy dishes to counteract the damp, misty dreariness of the evening. They chatted about what else could be done to protect Hobcaw Point, and Caitlin told Amanda about the planned series that her friend Beth was writing for the paper. The evening was going very pleasantly until Caitlin's cell phone rang.

"Hello, Mother. What is so important that you called me on my cell phone? Did someone die?"

"No, no, nothing is wrong, dear. I just met the most charming gentleman and I cannot wait for you to meet him. Nate Wyche is just five years older than you, has never been married, and is absolutely delightful."

Caitlin took a deep breath. She stared at the ceiling of the restaurant for a long, silent minute as her mother babbled on about how appealing she had found Nate Wyche to be. Finally, Caitlin managed to stop her mother's stream of words. "Mother, I've known Nate for years. Yes, he's charming. So is his partner, one of the Colleton boys. I attended their joining ceremony four years ago. He is not available."

"What do you mean, joining ceremony?" Harriet asked, partially offended and partially confused.

"Mother, Nate is gay and has a committed companion. That's one problem with this latest plan of yours. The other is more fundamental – the one you refuse to get into your brain. I'M GAY, MOTHER! Lay off the matchmaking." With that she hung up.

Everyone in the small restaurant looked at the obviously angry young woman sitting at the corner table, then quickly look away as her glare swept the room. "Okay," she spoke to the whole assembly in the small room. "Yes, I'm gay. Anybody got a problem with that?" Silence was the only response.

THAT EVENING, several of the city commissioners gathered together at a high-end bar in downtown Charleston. They each carried the papers that Amanda had distributed at Friday's meeting. The most critical page was the comparison that she had made of the advantages and risks offered by each site and the relative cost of preparation that each required.

"Miss Sherman says that we may never be able to build by the little harbor because of the cemetery on the site, right?"

"Yes. Caitlin Balle can stop us cold on that one point, even if Pinkney's eminent domain suit succeeds."

"And because of the silt in the harbor and the creek, not only will we spend a fortune on initial dredging, but we'll have to repeat it regularly to keep the channel clear?"

"That's what she says."

"And with the ruins from the old ship yard all over the place, the Historical Society may stop us cold as well."

"Yup."

"But by building the club facing onto the Wando, we avoid all this pain and all this cost?"

"Yup."

"What the hell is Pinkney's problem?"

"Damned if I know."

"So what do we do?"

Several drinks and three bowls of pimento cheese later, they still didn't have a clear plan to stop the chairman's obsession.

ON TUESDAY MORNING, the dredging barge was hauled into the creek by a small tug boat. The dredging crew spent the morning setting up to start clearing out the old harbor.

The Selkie, without his fur skin, and the Ghillie Dhu sat under the trees between the old harbor and the old dry dock, watching the burly, sweaty men struggle with the crane, various pipes, hoses, and other gear that they had to assemble to be able to begin dredging in the narrow space.

"Wonder how long it will take until one of them falls in?" Ronan grinned. He knew what was ahead for the dredgers.

"Well, they dinna hae anything to hang on to, so mayhap before lunch." Birch grinned.

"Should I go in to rescue them?"

"Nae, my friend. Let them wallow."

They continued to watch, making comments that ridiculed the clumsiness of the crew in the tight quarters for the rest of the morning.

Then the dredgers tried to figure out how to get the second barge in place so they could haul the dirt, mud, and detritus they sucked from the harbor out to sea to be dumped. The multiple failed attempts, and the inevitable need to reconfigure the dredging equipment had both Fae rolling on the ground laughing.

~

CAITLIN CAME HOME that evening intent on continuing her search for the missing deed, but somehow, something was missing. It was too quiet. The house was too empty.

"What is wrong with me? I LOVE this place. I love my solitude. It gives me time to think and relax."

She wandered into the library, sat down, and considered the next document box to be searched. Her eyes went from the box to the telephone, back to the box, then back to the phone.

'She promised to help. Perhaps if I called and asked, she'd come over,' but its supper time and I didn't get to the grocery store.' She thought for a minute. 'I could get something delivered. That new place down the street does a good chicken bog and delivers. If I order enough for two and she doesn't come over, I'll have dinner for tomorrow too.'

She picked up the phone and ordered chicken bog for a crowd. She waited until the food was delivered, since she wanted to have the chicken dish in one of her own pots and being kept warm on the back of the stove before Amanda came over – if she came over.

She picked up the phone again – this time a little hesitantly. Truth was, she wasn't just lonely; she was missing

Amanda. They had been together so often in the evenings that Caitlin felt the loss when she wasn't around.

"Hi, Amanda. Have you eaten yet?"

"No, I just got in, actually. Things were a little hectic today, with the dredging crew showing up. They went to start in the harbor, but when I got there, I told them to work on the creek first. That put a bit of a kink in the works."

"I'm sorry. You must be tired."

"Not so much tired as frustrated."

"Can I add to your frustration?"

"Oh, why not!"

"Come over and help me search. I'll feed you a lovely bowl of chicken bog and let you get miserably dusty."

"How can a girl pass up an offer like that? I'll be over after I've showered."

"Eh, come on over now – all you'll do is get dirty and dusty again and then you'll need another shower. Don't waste water, my friend."

"Cait, you want me to shower. I stink."

"A little girl stink never hurt anyone. Hey, if you're good, you can bring a change of clothes and stay over."

"I could be persuaded."

'Damn,' Caitlin thought. 'Could I be any more obvious?'

'Damn,' Amanda thought. 'She must really miss me.'

Amanda showed up about twenty minutes after their phone call. "Hi. I'm sweaty and dusty and hungry, but ready to slog through document boxes with you."

"Good. First, let's feed you. Grab whatever you want to drink out of the fridge while I serve up some bog."

"Bog?

"A chicken, sausage, and rice dish – one of the traditional low-country one pot meals. I think you'll like it."

Amanda took a taste of what looked like a theme and variation on arroz con pollo crossed with jambalaya. An expression of extreme pleasure came over her face as the unique flavor of bog filled her mouth. "Ummm." It was the only sound she could make and keep eating at the same time.

"I take it I've found another low-country dish that meets with your approval, oh mid-western meat and potatoes girl?" Caitlin grinned. "I suppose I'll have to keep tempting you with more goodies to keep you around, won't I?"

Amanda swallowed, shoveled in another mouthful, and nodded enthusiastically. It did not take long until Caitlin was serving up another helping of the chicken dish. She thought, 'Damned good thing I ordered several servings. Guess I won't have to worry about leftovers.'

The two women finished eating and straightened up the kitchen together. Caitlin then said, "I guess we need to get to it. Those papers are calling our names."

With fresh drinks to keep them going, they retreated to the library. Amanda climbed up the library ladder to retrieve the last two boxes on the top shelf to the right of the fireplace. Sitting Indian style on the floor, they started plowing through the collection of papers – receipts, orders, plans for maintenance activities on various ships, parts lists, lumber orders, and the unending detritus of the business of running a working shipyard.

"I suspect you've got the makings for a number of historical papers here, Cait – maybe even a book. If I were into doing research in engineering history, I might find enough material here to also publish."

"Well, for me, in the world of publish or perish, it's a gold mine."

They finished the first set of document boxes at about the same time. Amanda rose to collect another couple of boxes for them to go through. As she pulled one down, a heavy ledger fell against the back wall of the shelf. A rather hollow thud followed.

Siobhan grinned to herself. Moving anything in the physical world was difficult for her, but she had succeeded. Perhaps the clever engineer would get the hint.

Amanda looked at the shelf, a puzzled look on her face. The shelves should not sound hollow. A closer inspection showed her that the interior depth of the shelf was shallower than the outside would indicate.

She was about to examine the shelves more closely when the front door slammed – loudly. Caitlin and Amanda looked at one another, startled at the interruption. Caitlin knew she had locked the front door when she came in, and Amanda had come in through the kitchen. The only person who had a key was...

"MOTHER! What are you doing coming in unannounced and slamming doors like that?"

Harriet was in high dudgeon. "What am I doing? This was my husband's house; I have every right to be here whenever I want! And how dare you speak to me like that!"

"This is my house, according to the will, and you need not come stomping into MY house screaming at the top of your lungs."

"After the way you spoke to me last night, I have every right to come to teach MY DAUGHTER proper respect and manners!" Harriet shot back.

"What? I told you the truth, even though it's a truth you've been told repeatedly and refuse to accept."

"Truth? TRUTH? That my daughter is a pervert, one whose perversion will mean that after 350 years you will end the noble line of the Balles?"

"Mother, I am gay. I've been telling you that for years, and every time I've had a relationship with a woman, you've done your best to make sure it didn't work. You keep introducing me to every single man from an old Charleston family you can lay your claws into – regardless of whether they're rank alcoholics, womanizing philanderers, gold diggers, or twenty years older than me! Never EVER have you shown a moment of concern for my happiness! Not once. It has always been about social position and how you are seen in that crowd of old bigots you keep trying to be a member of."

Caitlin took a deep breath to try and get hold of her emotions.

Harriet looked like she'd been hit over the head with a two by four.

"All right, Mother. I'll say this in nice, simple words. I intend to have children, either through artificial insemination or by adoption. I've just turned twenty-eight. I have a good twelve years before child bearing will be a problem. When I find someone to spend my life with, someone who will give OUR children the love and care they deserve from two loving parents, then I will have at least one little Balle to continue the family line. Let me be perfectly clear to you. I will pick my partner. My partner will be a woman who I love and who loves me. You will have nothing to say in who I pick to be with. So stop the match making and harassment. The only thing I want from you at this point is for you to be happy for me when I find the right woman."

Caitlin stood there, panting from the intensity of emotion that she had expressed, so drained that she was no longer angry.

Amanda quietly walked up behind her friend and put her arm around Caitlin's shoulder.

Harriet looked at the two of them. If Caitlin had just grown two heads, she couldn't have looked more shocked. Without saying another word, she stalked out of the room, quietly let herself out the front door, and was gone.

Caitlin sagged against Amanda's side, drawing comfort from the honest offer of support. "Well," she mumbled, "that could have gone better, I think."

"I'm sorry you had to go through that. Come into the kitchen and I'll make you a cup of tea, and then you can either talk or just sit. I'll be here either way."

Siobhan watched them as Amanda helped a rather shaky Caitlin into the kitchen. "Well, I hope she remembers the hollow thump. I'd hate having to create another wad of ectoplasm."

THE SEARCH for the missing deed was forgotten as Caitlin absorbed the reality of what she had done when she confronted her mother that evening. She had loved her father, and Stephen had been a wonderful parent, teaching her, encouraging her, accepting her for who she was. Harriet had never been that kind of parent. Instead, she had seen to it that Caitlin went to cotillion, with its lessons in ballroom dancing and polite society manners, that she had always dressed in fashionable clothing, had the right toys, read the right books, went to the right parties and the best schools. Unfortunately, it also kept her from having a best friend, or a crowd that she could run around with who took her for herself. Her mother created a very lonely child, and after her father's death, a lonelier adult.

Once the gates of her sorrow and loneliness had been opened, there was no going back, no closing them. She poured her heart out; all the sadness, all the sense of being shut out from a real life, and all the determination to be her own woman and not her mother's fantasy; they all came out to Amanda's sympathetic ears and gentle, accepting heart.

It was sometime around midnight when Amanda realized that the following day was a work day. They both needed some proper sleep. Caitlin was curled against her shoulder; they were both half sitting, half lying on the sofa in the library, and Amanda's shirt was thoroughly damp from Caitlin's tears. Yet, even with the sorrow and pain that had been purged this evening, Amanda was happy to be holding the gentle woman who had opened her heart to her in her arms, safe from the pain of the night.

"Cait, honey. Are you awake?"

"No," she mumbled, her arms tightening around Amanda's waist and her head tucking against her shoulder more tightly.

"Cait, dear. Its past bedtime. Let me take you up and tuck you in."

"Only if you come with me."

"That can be arranged," Amanda said quietly.

"Okay."

They untangled themselves and Amanda pulled the tired woman from the sofa. She guided her gently up the stairs and into the master bedroom, where she pulled the covers down to wait for Cait. "Go on, brush your teeth, put on your nightgown, and I'll tuck you in, sweeting."

Caitlin dutifully wandered into the bathroom and shut the door. Amanda heard the sound of running water. She stepped across the hall to the guest room and quickly changed into the shorts and t-shirt she had brought with her to sleep in. By the time she returned to the master bedroom, Caitlin was just coming out of the bathroom.

"Let me brush my teeth and I'll tuck you in." Truth be told, Amanda's bladder needed attention more than her teeth did.

Emerging from the bathroom, Amanda came over to the side of the bed where Caitlin had settled herself in the center of the queen-sized mattress. She sat down and turned to Caitlin, smoothing an errant lock of hair off her forehead, then cupping her' cheek in her hand. "You've had a tough day, Cait. I'm glad I was able to be here for you. And if it helps at all, you did the right thing with your mother. What she was doing to you was cruel."

"I know, but she is my only living relative and it hurts to realize how alone I am."

"Cait, you aren't alone. If you look around, you have all sorts of people you can reach out to and they'll be there for you. You just need to let yourself reach out. And I'm here for you whenever you need me."

Caitlin closed her eyes, thinking about what Amanda was saying, but more importantly, savoring the feeling of her hand on her cheek. "In a small voice, she said, "Could you stay here tonight?"

"I thought that was already agreed on."

"No, I mean here. With me. I don't want to be alone tonight."

Amanda smiled gently, then crawled into bed and took the shaken woman into her arms. She found she liked it there in the bed as much as she had downstairs on the sofa.

"Rest easy, Cait. I'm right here." She kissed the top of the head cuddled into her shoulder, and settled in to sleep.

Morning came with gray light filtering into the bedroom. Amanda woke, accustomed to being up around sunrise, and found herself enclosed by a red-headed human octopus. She gently extracted herself, made a quick stop in the bathroom, and proceeded downstairs to make a pot of coffee. Even though Caitlin usually drank tea, this morning was definitely a coffee morning.

As the aroma of coffee made its way up the stairs, it drew a rather rumpled Caitlin; she was a woman in search of the blessed cup of caffeine. She looked at Amanda, who was leaning against the sink sipping her coffee, as she made a beeline for the coffee pot, poured a cup, and then leaned against the counter beside Amanda, close but not touching.

Amanda looked at her, smiling at the tousled, obviously embarrassed woman standing beside her. "Good morning. How you feeling this morning? Have you realized you're not alone yet?"

Caitlin put her coffee cup down on the counter and stared at the floor in front of her. In a small voice she started, "I want to apologize for dragging you into the middle of my family—"

Amanda stopped her right there, sliding one arm around her waist and laying the fingers of her other hand over her lips. "Stop right there. I am here because I want to be here. I want to be with you. Caitlin, I like you – a lot. I want to get this mess with Hobcaw Point under control, get the yacht club built over on the Wando River, perhaps turn the old shipyard into a historic site, and see what can happen between you and me. I like being with you. I like talking with you. I like doing things with you and going places with you. And frankly, I'd like to kiss you. I usually kiss a girl before going to bed with her, not that I've done either very often, but I'll take what I can get."

Caitlin looked into Amanda's eyes and saw nothing but honesty and a twinkle of humor at the last statement. "I do too, but like you, I'll take what I can get. Can I get that kiss now?"

It was a slow, gentle, tender kiss that promised more to come in the future. It went on for quite a while, until they broke apart to breathe again. "That was a lovely start, Cait, dear. Can we do it again tonight? Cause I have to get showered and get to work. I'm already running a little late."

"Absolutely. And you sure do a good job of reminding a girl that she's not alone."

RONAN WAS SITTING at the edge of the creek, hidden under some overhanging branches, watching as the dredging crew maneuvered their barges to start dredging the creek first. He smiled an evil little seal smile, his whiskers flicking to taste the wind currents.

He watched the dredgers work for several hours, pulling mud, shells, pieces of wood, and assorted miscellaneous items – beer cans, soda bottles, sunken bait buckets, plastic bags that looked something like jelly fish – in other words, all of the junk that ends up on the bottom of any body of water. Ronan slipped under the water, his strength as a swimmer far more than a match for the suction of the dredging rig. The suction hose was big enough to pick up bottles and cans, but a foot long, rusted iron ship's cleat, fed into the hose carefully, was going to do some damage.

Ronan quickly swam back to his place under the trees to watch. Within a few minutes, there was a loud CLANK. The dredging pump started making strange thudding noises as the blades tried to turn and couldn't. Smoke started to rise from the pump. The dredging crew leapt to shut down the engine that ran the pump, and started cursing – very creatively, Ronan thought.

The big gray seal slipped under the water and swam away from the barges. They wouldn't be doing any more dredging today – and probably not tomorrow.

"No, Miss Sherman. We won't be able to get the parts in until tomorrow, and it will take pretty much the whole day to break down the equipment, find out what caused the problem, and then rebuild the dredge."

Amanda sighed. One more accident, one more delay, one more contribution to the growing risk of cost overrun. It was going to be a miserable day. And she had to talk to Pinkney. He had to know about this problem.

Henry Pinkney slammed the phone down, cursing. How dare that woman tell him that these were the kinds of problems that one had to expect when working on a known historical site! She was supposed to make things go smoothly, go easily. The little harbor at Hobcaw Point was a natural site for what he wanted – to be the man who restored the nautical history of Hobcaw, a history that had made Charleston a leader in US nautical affairs. He wanted to be as respected and accepted as those people with the fancy names and the great big family trees. He wanted to show that snooty Harriet Smith that he was just as good, just as important as that wussy Stephen Balle she had married instead of him.

His secretary knocked and then came into his office without being invited. She set the morning mail in his inbox, then left again without a word. He knew what that meant – there was something in the mail that he didn't really want to see.

He flipped through the envelopes and found the one from the South Carolina Department of Archives and History. He just looked at the envelope, not wanting to open it but knowing he had to. With fingers shaking from anger, he opened the flap and pulled the letter out. It was what he was afraid of. That little bitch, Stephen's daughter, was petitioning to have the Hobcaw Point shipyard property officially placed on the National Register of Historic Places. If that happened, there would be all kinds of restrictions as to what could be built on the site. Even if the eminent domain suit to have the county take ownership was successful, and he knew it would be if the Balle bitch couldn't find the deed, he wouldn't be able to get through all the permissions needed to build on a registered site.

He had to get this done BEFORE the site was officially on the register.

He grabbed his jacket and keys and stomped out of the office. Miss Sherman was about to get an earful.

SAMUEL HEARD the car coming down the shell-covered road before it could be seen. In a moment, the obnoxious Cadillac pulled into the parking area and the fat, irritating man jumped out of the car and slammed the door, heading for the trailer with a grimly angry look on his face. Samuel called Grear and Kade. "Go. See if you can disable that disgusting silver monstrosity. I need to find out what he is about."

Samuel slipped into the trailer and watched as the fat man riffled through Amanda's papers, tools, and other items on the drawing table. 'He should not be messing with the Sherman woman's possessions. Perhaps a little something to discourage him.'

The phantom gathered himself, then wrapped his chilly ectoplasm around the fat man, trying his best to push the interloper away from the table.

Pinkney took a step back, a shiver running down his spine. He tried to step back up to the table, and again, that spine shaking chill hit him. It was like walking into a wall of ice. He looked at the air conditioner mounted in the wall at the end of the trailer. It must be the setting on the vents, so he walked over to the control panel and turned it off. Again, he tried to approach the drawing table. Again, he hit that wall of freezing air. So again, he backed off. He wasn't dressed for winter temperatures.

"Where is that dratted woman? She should have heard me coming and should be here by now." He glanced out the window and saw Amanda jogging up from where the harbor entered into the creek. "About time," he grumbled.

'Arrogant sleeveen!' Samuel thought. 'Have to admit my lady wife may be right about this lass, though. She is doing right by the shipyard, and the wife said she stood by our granddaughter in the face of that pitiful excuse for a woman that Stephen married.'

Pinkney stepped out of the trailer to hurry Amanda along. "Where were you? I'm supposed to be able to find you when I need you."

"Good morning, sir. I was down by the creek, talking with the dredging crew about what it will take to become operational again." Amanda drew a breath, since she had been jogging and was panting a bit. "In other words, sir, I was doing my job." She would not take any guff from this pompous little man. His temper tantrum at last Friday's meeting had seriously pissed her off.

"Well, I received notification today that makes it imperative that you progress as quickly as possible. Stick to your schedule. If you can come in early, there will be a nice bonus for you."

"I will do all that is required, both to meet engineering standards as required by my contract, and legally, as required by your state and county. I will not risk the welfare of our staff, nor will I damage any historical structures, per the law of this state. Beyond that, I will do the best I can."

"See that you do," the pompous little man said as he stomped back to his car.

'Good girl,' thought Samuel as he drifted back to his stone.

CHAPTER 7

THE CHARLESTON COUNTY COMMISSIONER FROM the Mt. Pleasant district stood in front of the desk of the county contracting manager. "So, did you track down the ownership of the property facing Hobcaw Creek and that facing out onto the Wando?"

"Yes, sir. That whole piece of land is owned by Caitlin Balle. While we have no property deed on file, all the plat maps and all the tax records going back to the late 1860s show the Balle family as the owners, and the taxes have always been paid on time. We have no records before about 1868 because many of them were destroyed during and immediately after the war."

"Do we have a legitimate claim that the property is abandoned?"

"Frankly, sir, deeds that date back to before the Civil War are few and far between. We have always used the tax records as the way to track ownership, and since the taxes are paid and the cemetery is evidently maintained, even though the property is not improved, it is not abandoned either. If they have a decent lawyer, we have no claim of eminent domain based on abandonment."

"What about eminent domain based on genuine necessity to take the property for public use?"

"Well, to be honest, if they have a good lawyer, building a yacht club, even if it is for public use, given that there are already several public use docks with facilities, and there are locations around the area that could be fairly purchased that would do just as well, I think a good lawyer could get this killed in court. Given that they're working to get the site put on the National Register of Historic Places, my best guess is that unless the judge has been seriously bought, this will fail in court."

The commissioner sighed. "They have a good lawyer – Spencer Rowe. I'm sure that part of his strategy is why they're working on the National Register listing." He thought for a minute. "So, why is Pinkney so set on this? Seems to me to be a major waste of county money."

The contracting officer rubbed her cheek. "If I had to guess, I'd say it was a personal thing. I went to school with young Caitlin's mother, Harriet Smith. Henry Pinkney used to follow her around like a lost puppy when we were in school. Harriet was a snob – I guess she still is – and wouldn't have anything to do with him. And we both know what kind of an ego that wannabe has."

"On a slightly different issue, I asked you to look at Miss Sherman's contract. If we chose not to build the yacht club, could we cut her loose?"

"She was hired to "perform civil engineering services for Charleston County" for the next three years. No projects were specified; just the nature of the work. So, we've got her for whatever we need her to do for the next two years and ten months before we can legitimately dump her without cause."

"That was a dumb contract – we always need a back door. Who... don't tell me – Pinkney approved it."

"Right in one."

"Okay. I'll take this to the board and see what we can do."

"While you're at it, you need to worry about the architect's contract, the dredging contract, and the construction company contract. No back doors there either."

"Thanks." He left the office, shaking his head and muttering, "Pinkney is an idiot."

WEDNESDAY MORNING DAWNED CLOUDY, muggy, and hot. Charleston in the summer was definitely not for the heat sensitive.

Amanda pulled into her usual parking space beside the trailer and was startled to see the silver Cadillac waiting for her. 'Hell, it isn't even 7:30 and he's already here. What now?'

She got out of her Jeep, grabbed her thermos of coffee and her briefcase, and walked over to the trailer. As she unlocked the door, Pinkney was right behind her.

"Good morning, Mr. Pinkney. What can I do for you today?"

"You can tell me what progress you've made."

"It's only been two days since you were last here. The

dredging barge should be back up and running by mid-morning, and the ground clearing is proceeding according to schedule."

"I need more progress than that. I want you to start clearing these old ruins."

Amanda stood silently for a moment, looking at the papers on her drawing table. She then turned around slowly to look at Pinkney. "Sir, until the title to this property is clearly in the hands of Charleston County, to remove any structure without the permission of the owner would be illegal. The county has the right to clear the underbrush as it offers a habitat for creatures that could be harmful for the citizenship. Similarly, we have the right to dredge the creek, as the county holds the rights to the waterways, but if I were to authorize removal of any structure on this property, even ruins of previous structures, it would be deemed at minimum vandalism and trespassing, and would place the county at risk for a nasty lawsuit and it would put my license at risk, neither of which I will do."

Pinkney's face turned an ugly shade of red as he listened to Amanda's response.

Before he could say anything, Amanda added to his frustration. "So, how is the eminent domain action going?" She knew full well that Mr. Rowe had petitioned for and obtained an extension on the court cases to give Caitlin time to find the deed. "I think you should also look into the implications of this property being placed on the National Register. It may have an impact on what you can build here."

Pinkney sputtered. "Alright. Keep doing whatever is legal to do – but be ready to jump into action to clear this place for construction as soon as I get that title cleared. If you are not ready, I will see to it that your contract is terminated."

"I'm not sure you can do that, since I will have done all that was legally possible and the contract does not specify the project I am to perform. I serve at the county's direction within that which is legal." She paused for a moment. "And I suggest you consider the property over at the outlet into the Wando River – if the Historical Society has its way, that will be your best option."

"Thank you for that information, Miss Sherman." He stomped away, got into his car, slammed the door and drove away.

Pinkney pulled into his garage and let himself into the kitchen, annoyed that his wife had forgotten to set the alarm – again. He thought Sherry had already left; she had some sort of garden club event that morning. So, he was surprised when she walked out of the bedroom, half dressed.

"Henry, what are you doing here? I thought you'd left for work."

"I did, but I remembered I have a casual lunch today and I'm overdressed, so I came home to change."

"Oh, of course. We can finish dressing together."

"Much as I'd like to, um, make it a slow process, I really need to get going. Busy, busy, busy."

"You're always busy," Sherry pouted.

While Sherry was in the bathroom doing her makeup, he made a quick call.

"Judge Joseph Monk's office. How can I help you?"

"Tell him that Hank Jones needs to talk to him, please." Jones was his father's last name before he changed it.

"Hello, Hank. What is so urgent?"

"We need to talk. We may have a problem or two."

"Shall I meet you for lunch? Usual place."

"I'll be there."

Pinkney pulled on a polo shirt and a pair of Sansabelt slacks, slipped his feet into a pair of loafers, and looked like any one of a thousand tourists that wandered around Charleston's old town.

He walked back into the kitchen and poured himself a cup of coffee from the pot that had been made earlier in the morning. He picked up the newspaper and started scanning through it as he sipped his coffee. There on the top of the style section was a headline he did NOT want to see; *Charleston's First Shipyard,* and in smaller letters, *Hobcaw Point Helped Put the Port of Charleston on the Map.* The byline for the article was one Elizabeth Dauntry. There was a wide-angle picture of the ruins of the main house.

He threw the paper down on the table, cursing. He picked the paper back up and the cursing got louder and louder as he continued to read. By the time he got to the end of the article and noted that there would be another article about the history of shipbuilding in Charleston the following day, he was sweating, cursing, and stomping his feet.

Sherry came into the room, dressed and ready to go to her morning event. She knew better than to say anything to Henry when he was in this kind of mood.

Pinkney noticed her, and threw her his car keys. "Take the Caddy. I want to take the Prius today. Need to look environmentally friendly."

With that, he walked out the door, into the garage, stomped over to the car, and pulled out of the garage.

Sherry looked after him. "Hummm. I didn't know you could squeal the tires of a Prius."

Pinkney stomped into the offices of the Post and Courier. The young woman at the reception desk looked up at him and smiled a plastic smile that never reached her eyes. "How can I help you, sir?"

"I am Henry Pinkney. I need to see your managing editor."

"Let me see if Mr. Abrams is available, Mr. Pinkney."

Pinkney paced around the lobby waiting for Abrams to appear. That article in the paper would do nothing but place focus on the historic aspects of the damned site, and until he could get the title issue cleared up, anything that brought the historical societies in the town would be an invitation to get the damned site on the register, and that would mean he would not be allowed to build his beautiful yacht club.

A tall gray-haired man in shirt sleeves and an open collar walked up to him. "Mr. Pinkney, I'm Adam Abrams. To what do I owe the pleasure of your company?"

"I would like to know what inspired you to run that article on the Hobcaw Point site. There are some issues that are in the court system now and some might view that article as inflammatory." Pinkney was ready to spit nails, but as a politician, knew enough to not completely blow his top at the head of the most widely read newspaper in Charleston.

"Mr...? Ah, yes, Pinkney. Aren't you one of the county commissioners? Well, never mind. The Charleston Museum is building a new exhibit on pre-revolutionary life in Charleston, and we understand that Hobcaw Point may be put on the National Register because it was the first shipyard in Charleston. I know there are ruins out there, and I appreciate the irony that there's an engineer who's looking at it, Miss Amanda Sherman, who is a descendant of the man who ordered it burned down. All in all, it's a good, solid local interest story. Does that answer your question?"

There was nothing in Abrams's reasons for running the story that couldn't be easily found in the local news or public records, nothing about the planned yacht club, and nothing to link the interest to either Amanda Sherman or Caitlin Balle. Yet, Pinkney somehow had a feeling that at least one and maybe both women had initiated this journalistic interest.

"Thank you, Mr. Abrams. Since I represent Mt. Pleasant, I am always curious when the journalistic eye is turned toward my neighborhood. Have a good day, sir." Pinkney turned and strolled out of the lobby, trying to look calm and controlled and seething inside.

THE GROUND CREW foreman knocked on Amanda's door.

She was sitting at her drafting table, where she had a detailed map of the site, and was filling in all of the findings her crew had made as they worked to clear the property of underbrush. She had lightly penciled in the buildings noted in the pre-revolutionary map, and as her crew found more foundations, she solidified the lines for the building remains they found. She was focused on the drawing and didn't register him knocking for a moment. Finally, it dawned on her that someone was looking for her.

"Come in," she called.

"Miss Amanda, we've found more foundations."

"Show me."

He went to the map and indicated a mid-sized building already penciled in on the drawing. "Looks like we've found the one labeled as the sail maker's loft."

"There may be a load of artifacts around it, some of them small, so be careful, mark anything you find, and bring it to me. I'll have a detailed grid map for you as soon as I can."

The foreman grinned. "I'll wait. It's good to be out of the heat. So, are we groundsmen or are we becoming archeologists, boss lady?"

"I think a little of both, Buddy." She pulled her laptop to her and pulled up an image of the plat map, and zeroed in on the area his crew was working on that day. She expanded the image and overlayed a charting grid and the pencil sketch from the old map for him.

He grinned as she printed his grid map. "See ya later."

Amanda finished updating the large graph on her drawing table, then unrolled another representation of the property and started evaluating it for water flow patterns, so she could begin looking at what would have to be done to direct the water from heavy rain storms from damaging things. Hydraulics had never been her favorite subject, so she was being particularly careful with this work.

At a little after ten o'clock, Amanda was disturbed by another knock on the trailer door. Absently, she called "Come in," assuming it was Buddy with something else from the area around the sail maker's loft. It wasn't.

"Good morning, Miss Sherman," called Sarah Highsmith. "I hope we're not disturbing you, since we just came out without calling first, but we wanted to see the site as soon as possible."

"Dr. Highsmith, you are always welcome. What can I do for you?" She stood up from her drawing table to greet the visitors and shake hands all around.

"I'd like you to meet Daniel Amy, Helen Sothel, and Nate Wyche, all from the Historical Commission. We'd like to look around the site and help these nice folks determine if it is worthy of inclusion on the National Registry. If you're right about the site, they are the folks we will need to deal with to obtain a restoration grant."

"A pleasure, folks. Can I get you anything before we go tramping around? I have some reasonably fresh coffee." Thank God, she'd finally brought in a decent coffee maker. No more instant crap.

"No, thank you. We had coffee just before we came out."

"Well then, let me show you the site map first, then we can go look at what we've found."

They gathered around her table as she cleared the hydraulic information to the side. "Here is a plat map of Hobcaw Point as it is today." She pulled out a copy of the old site drawing. "Here is a pre-revolutionary drawing of the site that was provided by the Balle family from their records and has been verified to be consistent with the date on the drawing. I have compared the known ruins to the original map, and so far, have validated the presence of foundation ruins for a number of the buildings, either through actual discovery of the foundation stones as we cleared the undergrowth or by conducting sounding using metal probes. As a matter of fact, our ground crew found the foundations of the sale maker's loft just this morning. Buildings that we have identified are drawn into the master plan in black ink and properly labelled; those that we suspect to exist but have not yet verified are in pencil."

She stepped back and let the team of historians look over the results of her meticulous findings.

When they started looking around the office, Amanda motioned to the table at the end of the trailer. "These are the artifacts that we've found as we pulled weeds and vines up. Most were tangled in the roots, though that cleat tried to destroy the dredging machine when it was sucked up into the vacuum pump." She pulled out a file folder and laid it on the table with the artifacts. "As you can see, we've tagged everything and mapped the location were we found them in these documents."

Nate Wyche looked at Amanda closely. "I understood you were an engineer, Miss Sherman. From the looks of things, you're as much an archeologist as an engineer."

"I'm a civil engineer, which is a bit different from people who design equipment. Our job is to convert an architect's ideas into physical reality. We learn how to deal with the earth that will provide the foundation for buildings, infrastructure, and landscaping. One of the things we learn is how to take care of artifacts that may provide historical or forensic information."

"Well, it looks to me as if you and your crew have made an excellent start here. This site looks like a veritable gold mine of historical information." The other members of the committee nodded in agreement.

Miss Sothel looked at Amanda, liking what she saw. She was a friend of Sarah's and, like the rest of the committee, family as well as being an old school South Carolinian. "Shall we go look at the real thing?"

"Glad to. Good. You've all worn boots. I still don't trust tromping around here without them. We've found several nests of baby copperheads, enough so I keep anti-venom on hand. Shall we start at the main house and go from there?"

The four committee members nodded and they started the trek around the property. They were duly impressed with the care that Amanda and Buddy had taken with each of the discovered foundations around the property. She also took them over to the mud flat where they had flags posted outlining the dry dock.

Finally, Mr. Amy pointed to the huge old live oak tree that stood beside the old cemetery, close enough to be imposing but far enough away so the roots wouldn't disturb the coffins beneath the ground. "Tell me, Ms. Sherman, how much work did your crew have to do to put this cemetery in such good shape?"

"Oh, no, we didn't do anything here. The family has caretakers who come in every week to trim and weed, and one of the family members comes in at least every month to make sure it's properly tended."

"In your professional opinion, this property has not been abandoned?"

"While the land is not improved, it has not been abandoned based on the care taken to maintain this part of the property. I don't understand why you're asking this, Mr. Amy."

"Well, it seems that the county administrators are claiming the property is abandoned and that justifies their taking ownership."

"I am aware of the situation with the courts, sir. As a result, I have limited the actions taken here on the property to those that can be legitimately taken by the county with regard to unimproved property. My crew and I have been meticulous in not doing anything that would damage or destroy any of the relics, artifacts, or structures on the property and have further discussed this caution with Mr. Pinkney as the contracting supervisor from the county. I'll await the decision of the court before my crew does anything further."

"Commendable, Miss Sherman. Very commendable."

A TALL, light skinned black man, dressed in jeans and a t-shirt, was leaning against the base of the USS Maine's capstan in the middle of the Battery Park, eating an ice cream cone. Pinkney, in his polo shirt and Sansabelt pants, looked like any one of a dozen middle aged tourists wandering around. The black man didn't look at Pinkney, who leaned against the concrete block around the corner from him, but asked tersely, "So, what's the problem that has you in a twist?"

"The damned engineer isn't willing to bend the rules, the Historical Commission is involved now, the damned Balle girl has one of the best lawyers in town, and it looks like the property's going to be put on the National Register. Which means all our lovely little plans for making a buck or two off the construction are going down the drain."

"The case will come to my court. You have to trust that I'll do the necessary. You and I have too much at stake here."

"Are you going to be able to overrule whatever Spencer Rowe brings to the table?"

"Depends – there's no love lost between him and me. If I go too far over the line, Rowe will take me to the Bar. So I'll have to be careful and support everything I do with precedents."

"Be sure you do. We've got a hell of a lot riding on this. And the article in the paper this morning isn't going to help."

"All right. Watch your step. I'll watch mine."

THE SANDY-HAIRED MAN in the pale gray summer-weight suit stepped into Spencer Rowe's office without knocking, walked up behind him, leaned down and kissed the back of his neck. "Hello, sweetheart."

"DAVE! What are you doing here? You never come to my office... unless it's on official business. This is official business, isn't it?"

"Well, sweetheart, it's sort of quasi-official business. I know you're Caitlin's lawyer – and I'm pretty sure you're gonna quash this ridiculous B.S. that Pinkney's trying, so if Caitlin's title to the land is clear and clean, do you think she'd be willing to sell the county part of that land – the part that faces the Wando?"

"You know I can't talk about an active case – especially with you, since you're a commissioner."

"Oh, I'm not asking you to talk about it with me. I'm asking you to talk about it with Caitlin. And figure out a price for the land. We want the yacht club, but not on the shipyard site – over on the Wando, where there aren't any ruins to worry about and where we won't have to dredge up half the mud on the Point."

"I think I can do that for you, but first we have to get the title clear."

"My love, I have every faith that you will pull that one off without even breaking a sweat."

"You fool. Now, since it's getting to be quitting time, why don't I buy you some dinner?"

"Aren't you afraid we'll be accused of inappropriately consorting with the enemy?"

"We'll go somewhere that they know we're not enemies. Should we go pick up Davie first?"

AMANDA SHOWED up at Caitlin's door promptly at six o'clock, hot, sweaty, dusty, uninvited, and grinning like a Cheshire cat.

Caitlin had been home long enough to shed her shoes and change into shorts and a tank top. She had just poured a glass of iced tea when there was a knock on the back door. She peaked out of the window and saw the dusty Jeep sitting in the driveway and knew who it was. She yanked the door open and said, "Get in here, you sweaty mess." She thrust the glass into Amanda's hand while aiming her at the kitchen table.

"I had to come tell you about today's adventures."

"Okay, but drink your tea, cool down, catch your breath, and then tell me."

Amanda took a large swig of tea, then grinned at Caitlin.

"Do you know Daniel Amy, Helen Sothel, or Nate Wyche? They came and visited me, along with Sarah today."

"Hell, yes. I know all of them. They're all members of the Historical Commission."

"At a guess, they're all gay too. I think Sarah's created a Caitlin Balle support team."

"What happened?"

Amanda recounted her day in great detail, offering site by site commentary from the tour she'd conducted that day. "Of particular importance was Nate Wyche asking about the maintenance of the cemetery as proof that the property wasn't abandoned; it just wasn't improved."

"Do you think they're going to put it on the National Register?"

"I have absolutely no doubt of it."

"Well, that will certainly screw up Pinkney's plans, won't it?"

"It will."

"What about you? You were depending on this job."

"Well, seems that Pinkney screwed up my contract. I'm here for three years. The contract wasn't for the Hobcaw Point project; it was to be the civil engineer for Charleston County. So, unless I do something really egregious, I'm here for a while."

"And the yacht club? Doing the build on that would have made your career."

"I recommended they build the thing over on the shore of the Wando. Some guy named Gibbs, one of the other commissioners, seemed real interested."

Caitlin started laughing. "Dave Gibbs is Spencer's

partner. I went to their joining ceremony several years ago. So we have another alley."

"There's one thing that all of this depends on – you having clear title to the property."

Caitlin sighed. "I know. We need to keep looking."

Amanda agreed. "Food, then back to it."

Siobhan watched them shaking her head. What would it take for the damned engineer to get a hint?

CHAPTER 8

"You fucking asshole! You Goddamned FUCKING asshole!" Joseph Monk was stalking up and down Henry Pinkney's home office.

Monk had been waiting at the house for him when he came in from an after-work reception at the Chamber of Commerce that evening.

"What is the problem, Joe? Work is proceeding at the site, the dredging is going forward, and the Sherman woman hasn't caused any problems."

Monk took Pinkney's lapels in his hands and brought the little man within a few inches of his enraged face. In a very low, tight voice, Monk said, "The problem, you little shit, is that you clearly didn't understand how to use the law, and bright and early Monday morning, Spencer Rowe filed enough motions against your eminent domain efforts to stop you in your tracks for YEARS!"

"But... but you're the judge. You can throw them out."

"I'm a judge, and if anyone figures out our relationship,

I'll have to recuse myself. And quite honestly, if I throw some of these motions out, Rowe will have me up in front of the Bar Association in a New York minute. He has grounds, and a hellish collection of folks who will testify for that little Balle girl."

"So, what are we going to do?"

"I don't know yet. What I do know is if you don't find that chest, all this will be worthless."

"Are you really sure it's there?"

"My grandfather's grandfather was the captain's valet. He stayed in the area after the war was over and kept watch on the site. If someone had retrieved it, he would have known. The family has watched that site since then. In fact, some of them worked for the Balle family just so they could keep an eye on it."

"Why didn't someone retrieve it immediately after the ship yard was burned?"

"Well, for starters, the only survivor was my grandpa. The ship and docks burned to the waterline. The ship sank. It was only about ten feet deep, but still, it was hard to get to because of the debris from the fires. Then in 1867, a hurricane hit and started covering the wreckage with layers of mud. Getting to it just wasn't possible. I'm sure it's still there, under the mud flats."

"All right. So it's still out there under the mud flats."

"I'm sure of it."

"Let me see if I can figure something out. I'll talk with the dredger captain – he and I went to school together."

"You do that. You do whatever you need to do to get that chest. 'Cause I'm telling you now, the county isn't going to get that property; Spencer Rowe will see to it. If I were you,

I'd let them move the yacht club site over to the Wando. That way, Sherman will focus on that property and you'll be able to do more at the Hobcaw shipyard site."

"Okay, okay. I get it. Let me see if Sammy can suction the mud flats out."

"You do that – preferably quietly."

"Maybe we can figure out where the ship's hull is and just suction the target area."

"Harumph," Monk replied. "Do what you need to do, but find that trunk."

AMANDA AND CAITLIN were having dinner together again. Dinner on Wednesday and Saturday were becoming regular events for them. Other nights occurred when their schedules permitted. This Wednesday, they had walked about four blocks north of Caitlin's house to a rather modern but casual seafood and oyster restaurant.

"Seafood again? I've clearly converted you to low-country food." Caitlin laughed when Amanda suggested they return to the nearby source of all kinds of marine proteins.

"You certainly have, Miss Balle," laughed Amanda.

Amanda and Caitlin hadn't seen each another since Saturday evening. They each had commitments on Sunday – Caitlin to the museum and Amanda had been asked to meet with Commissioner Gibbs to show him around the entirety of Hobcaw Point without Pinkney's presence.

"How is your week going?" Caitlin asked.

"So far, so good. I haven't seen Pinkney for a week –

which always brings joy to my life. The dredgers keep finding little things out of the canal, so I think we should talk with Sarah about sieving the dredged mud from the canal and absolutely from the little harbor."

"What kind of things are you finding?"

"Oh, all kinds of things. Old mugs, ship fittings, a few coins, that kind of thing."

"Nothing big enough to mess up the dredging equipment again?"

"Not yet, but I suspect it's only a matter of time." She took another slurp of oyster. "How about you?"

"Spencer called. He dumped a load of motions on Judge Monk's desk Monday. He said he thought he had Pinkney by the short hairs, and just getting through the stuff he dumped on the court should slow things down enough for Sarah to get it on the register, which will end the visions of the yacht club for good."

"I am collecting and tagging everything we find for the Historical Commission."

"Good." Caitlin took on a spoonful of shrimp and grits and thought for a minute. "Spencer said we really need to find the deed if we can – if it even still exists – if not for the court, then for the history."

"If it's there, we'll find it sooner or later."

"It's later that scares me."

They strolled back to Caitlin's that night and spent a couple of hours wading through documents before Amanda headed back to her apartment, wishing she wasn't.

SAMUEL SAT ON HIS STONE, brooding. He was waiting for Grear and Kade to show up and let him know what that repellent little interloper Pinkney was up to. The two brownies were the most mobile, least perceptible of the Fae of Hobcaw Point. Their task was to keep track of what Pinkney was up to, as Siobhan had finally convinced Samuel that Amanda was not the destructive force her grandfather had been and the real threat was coming from the obnoxiously nouveau riche pipsqueak.

The two little imps appeared under the oak tree, eager to report to their laird.

"What say you, my friends?" greeted Samuel.

"I say that trying to follow that doolally around town to find out what his intents are is a journey. Me feet are killing me!" Kade sat down, pulled his boots off, and rubbed his feet to emphasize his point.

"What did you expect?" Samuel snorted.

"Well, this town has certainly grown, and riding under the hood of that big metal carriage is right miserable – hot, smelly, and things that go round and threaten to chop of yer haid."

"Weel, fer the most part, he was just his usual obnoxious self – a proper dobber to most he met. But there was one – a dark man who made our gowk into a proper feartie, scrapping like a scabby yaw."

"And what said this dark man?"

"That when the evil general burned down the place, there was a ship that was carrying a load of gold that burned and sank – and the gold was ne'er recovered. That's what they're looking fer."

"Aye, now makes more reason." Samuel looked

thoughtful. "If a ship was docked and burned to the waterline, t'would be neath the mud now." He stroked his beard. "I think we have a little disruption to create. And a grandchild to enrich."

Grear looked up, grinning. "I think I found a good way to distract the sorry roaster. Seems to be that he's a cuckhold as well as an eejit. That pink obsessed floozie o' his has found herself a younger stud ta play with."

"Oh, yes, shall we deprive him of the gold AND the doxie? I think so."

ON THURSDAY, after yet another night of dinner and document searching with Caitlin, Amanda made a major decision. Her contract ran for a full three years, so unless she was fired, she was going to be here for a while. Caitlin couldn't complain about her moving around every few months. She loved the area, the food ,and (mostly) the people here. Most importantly, she was falling and falling hard for the red-haired, freckle-faced little historian with the quiet manners and the solid steel spine.

She decided it was time for a real date. Flowers, dinner, dancing maybe, a romantic walk through the park in the moonlight, dressed in something other than khaki shorts, a polo shirt and sneakers.

Since her knowledge of Charleston nightlife was limited to politically correct events she had attended as the city's new civil engineer or places that Caitlin had introduced her to – and those were all pretty much all low-country casual – which she had discovered were so casual as to include bathing suits and t-shirts that had seen better days ten years before – she needed help in planning something romantic.

She called Sarah.

Sarah answered on the third ring, sounding a little breathless. "Highsmith. How can I help you?"

Rather timidly, Amanda answered. "Hi, Sarah. It's Amanda Sherman."

"Oh, hi, Amanda. Is there a problem out at the site I need to know about?"

"Uh, no, no, everything is all right here. I have some more artifacts that I've tagged and documented, but that's not why I called."

"Okaaayyyy?"

"I called to ask a personal favor, if you don't mind."

"If I can help, I will. I think you know that."

"Well, you see, um, I want to take someone out for a date – you know, dinner, dancing, that sort of thing...."

"Yeessss?"

"And, well, I don't know my way around Charleston and I hoped you could make some recommendations."

"Can I ask who? Or don't I need to?"

"Well, I thought I'd ask Caitlin. We've been seeing each another casually – you know, as friends, nothing romantic, but..." Amanda broke off, feeling both embarrassed and somewhat helpless.

"You want to woo the girl. Do I have that right?"

Gulp. "Yes," she whispered.

Sarah could hear how nervous Amanda was and had to struggle to keep from laughing. She was perfectly aware of Caitlin's lack of a love life and found it charming that the somewhat shy Yankee wanted to properly court the woman of the old South. "So, we need a restaurant, a decent dance club, a good florist?"

"That would be good," Amanda croaked.

"How about clothes for you?"

"Well, I have the suits I wear for business meetings."

"No, no. That won't do. Charlestonians like to dress up – as long as the clothing is cool." Sarah thought for a moment. "What are you doing this afternoon – can you take off?"

"I guess," Amanda murmured.

"Good. I'll pick you up about one – we'll have lunch, chat, and then go shopping."

"Shopping?"

"Yes. Shopping. If you're gonna do this, you need to look the part, girl. I'll see you in a couple of hours." Without further comment, Sarah broke the connection.

Amanda sat there, staring out the window, seeing nothing. "Shopping," she moaned.

PINKNEY WALKED into the shack on the dock that served as the dredging company's office. A tall, scruffy man wearing ancient, formless jeans, rubber boots, and a wife beater that once upon a time had been white but was now a variegated collection of stains in multiple shades of brown and red, carrying the history of Charleston area mud flats in its coloring, was waiting for him.

"Good afternoon, Raymond. I was hoping to catch you alone."

"What do you need this time, Pinkney?" Raymond wasn't noted for his manners.

"I need you to do some dredging without raising any attention."

Raymond's eyebrows went up. "What do you mean, attention?"

I need you to do it when that Sherman woman isn't around."

"That would be nights and weekends – and it's gonna cost you a chunk of change."

"I don't care. Look at this map."

He pulled out a plat map with the location of the old docks and the shape of a ship's hull sketched in.

"Shit, Pinkney, this is under the mud flats."

"I know. I need you to clear the bow of this boat."

"And you think I can do that without Ms. Sherman noticing?"

"I don't care if she notices after the fact. Just clear it quick and clean. Run shifts if you have to." He pulled an envelope out of his back pocket. "Here's five to get you started."

Raymond's eyebrows went up even higher. "I hope you mean five thousand."

"Yes, yes, and there's more where that came from if you get the job done quickly."

"I can't do it this weekend. I'll have to pull together a special crew. I can probably start next Friday."

THURSDAY EVENING, Amanda cleaned up after work, dressed as neatly as her wardrobe allowed, and went over to Caitlin's, bearing a bouquet of roses and a written invitation. She walked up to the door, started to knock, stopped and stepped back a step, stepped back up and finally knocked.

Caitlin opened the door, surprised to see Amanda there on a Thursday. Their regular days were Wednesday and Saturday. She looked into her friend's rather pink face, but Amanda was looking down at her feet.

It had been over four years since Amanda had asked anyone out for a real date. She was always a bit shy, and she was terrified that Caitlin would refuse her. The night she'd spent holding Caitlin after the break with her mother had not been repeated and Amanda hadn't seen anything other than friendship in Caitlin's words or actions. Maybe Caitlin had changed her mind, but Amanda was willing to forge on; they had talked briefly about wanting to know what was possible. Well, this was possible.

"I came by to ask, um..."

"Silly woman, come inside. There's fresh limeade in the box."

Obediently, Amanda followed Caitlin into the kitchen. "Here, I brought these for you. I thought you needed something to brighten your week."

"Oh, Amanda! They're lovely. Let me get a vase."

Amanda stood there, smiling gently as Caitlin arranged the bouquet of pink, white, green and golden roses, tulips, lilies, and things Amanda didn't know the names of in a crystal vase.

"I think I'll put these in the library where I can look at them while I work."

"That makes sense."

Amanda sipped her tea while Caitlin carefully snipped stems and arranged the flowers. "There. I think that will do."

"It's lovely," Amanda mumbled.

"So," Caitlin turned to look at her friend. "You wanted to ask me something?"

"Um, yes, well," Amanda took a deep breath. "I wanted to ask if you would go out with me on Saturday."

Caitlin frowned, looking confused. "Of course. We usually go out on Saturday."

"No, I mean go out with me." Amanda was blushing now.

Caitlin looked at her for a minute, then whispered, "You mean like on a date?"

"Yes, on a date," Amanda confirmed softly.

Caitlin smiled gently. This was a side of Amanda she hadn't seen before and was very happy to discover. "I would be honored and thrilled to go on a date with you. What time and how should I dress?"

"Well, shall I pick you up at seven and we can go from there? Nothing too fancy, no cocktail dresses, and you don't have to wear stockings, but something nice, please. I have reservations at a nice restaurant, and I want us to have a nice, relaxing evening without worrying about deeds and papers and pushy county commissioners." Amanda cringed inwardly – nice was a word she was clearly overusing. She shifted her focus back to her half empty glass of limeade.

Caitlin looked at the woman who had proven herself to be a friend and was now behaving like a teenaged boy asking a girl to the prom. It was cute, endearing, and entirely unnecessary. After all, Caitlin had spent one of the more difficult nights of her life in this woman's arms seeking comfort in a lonely world.

She walked over to Amanda and slid her fingers under her chin, lifting her head so she could look into those gentle brown eyes. "Darlin', you don't have to be shy or scared. I love the time we spend together, and I would go anywhere and do anything you wanted to do to spend time with you. I'll be ready on Saturday." She bent and placed a gentle kiss on Amanda's cheek.

The two of them just looked at one another for a moment, then Amanda said, "Since I'm here anyway, wanna go get some dinner and then slug through some more documents?"

"Sure – if I can tease you about dating. You realize that's what we've been doing on a sort of low level now for weeks?"

Amanda gulped. "You can – and I know we have. I thought we could take it up a level or three."

"You romantic, you."

WHEN SPENCER ROWE arrived at his office on Friday morning, he found a delegation of people waiting for him. The folks from the Historical Commission were starting to chafe at the bit, wanting to finalize the Hobcaw shipyard site on the register, but not wanting to mess up the court case for Caitlin.

Daniel Amy was acting as the spokesperson for the team. "So, what is going on with Hobcaw? I saw you filed a boatload of motions on Monday, but has Monk acted on any of them?"

"Not yet. We're scheduled to be in court over them on Wednesday morning."

"Do you want us there?"

"Couldn't hurt." Stephen grinned.

"Do you want us to go ahead with the register?"

"I probably will before this is over, and definitely before Monk gives Hobcaw to the county, but for right now, let's see what happens."

"Okay. Can we go back out and look at whatever else Ms. Sherman has found?"

"By all means – all it can do is strengthen the historical site story."

"Okay, Spencer. We'll do whatever else we can to help Caitlin out."

"Pull some strings and get this moved to another judge." Spencer laughed. He and Joe Monk were not the best of buddies.

The historians left the office and Spencer immediately picked up his phone. "Caitlin – it's Spencer. I just had a visit from the Historical Commission folks. They're gonna get Hobcaw onto the register, but please, please find that deed if you can."

"I'm doing my best, Spencer. You should see the library – I'm more than halfway through looking at every book, ledger, and document in there and still nothing."

"Well, keep looking, kiddo."

∾

THE HISTORICAL COMMITTEE showed up at Amanda's trailer door shortly after eleven. Helen Sothel had considerately brought sandwiches, fruit, and cookies for everyone.

The committee members started by going through the items that Amanda had found and catalogued. They then moved out, heading directly to the foundations of the main house.

It was a long, hot, messy, dirty, and eventually, muddy afternoon, as the dirt and dust mixed with their sweat to form reddish gray streaks on the arms, legs, and faces of the whole team. On the other hand, Amy, Sothel, and Wyche were ecstatic over the collection of items they had found – without doing any real digging. Amanda carefully documented eighteen coins from the seventeenth century, assorted buttons, the hilt of an old butter knife, a sadly battered soup spoon, a pair of sugar tongs, and assorted pieces of pottery shards.

The team returned to the trailer, as all findings needed to be kept in the trailer until the site became a formal archeological dig site, but the three historians were grinning like a pack of dust-streaked meerkats that had found a large nest of lizard eggs.

Amanda could not help herself. She was laughing as she told the muddy threesome her observation of their condition, then apologized. "I have to confess I watch too many shows on Animal Planet."

"Wait till we get into those mud flats. Your map shows dockage under one of the flats, and potentially a dry dock under the other. When we start in there, you'll be hard pressed to tell us from the mudskippers that inhabit those tunnels." Daniel Amy grinned evilly, his teeth glowing starkly white within his mud-smeared face. "You may take that as a threat!" They all laughed.

Amanda provided a pile of towels for them to at least partially clean themselves up in the small bathroom in the trailer, and sent them on their merry way.

Amanda packed up for the day. She hadn't gotten any of her own work done, but had a great time playing with the diggers. It soothed her sense of justice that Pinkney's project was clearly going to become a site on the National Register – and therefore all of his plans would be up in smoke. Once on the register, nothing could be built on the site that was not appropriate to the era of the original buildings.

She made it home in one piece, glad that she wasn't fighting the traffic that was heading east to the beaches for the weekend. The Cooper River Bridge eastbound was bumper to bumper and moving only slightly faster than snails. She stripped her muddy clothes off as she closed the door to her apartment, leaving her boots on the tiled entry way, and dropped her sweat-soaked shirt before she made it to the living room. As she started to slip her shorts off, her phone rang.

"Hello," she grunted as she continued to undress.

"Hi. I hate to bother you, but could you come over this evening and help me search? Spencer called today and basically ordered me to find that damned deed. Please?" Caitlin's whimper was somewhere between begging and whining.

"Caitlin, let me get a shower and I'll be right over. Should I pick up something for supper?"

"No, I'll get something. Just get here."

CAITLIN LEANED against the desk and looked around at the office – at the piles of papers and books, at the mess that her house had become – and was overwhelmed with a sense of futility. Her mother hated her, she had no family, no one in her life. And now that little slimeball Pinkney was trying to take away the one thing she could hang on to – her sense of family, the tradition and legacy that the Balle family had held onto through war, through the depression, through everything for over three hundred years. It had all gotten to her.

She slowly slid down to the floor, silent tears slipping down her cheeks. She sat there, silent, lost.

She didn't hear the knock on the back door when Amanda arrived.

Amanda knew she was home and let herself in the unlocked door. She found her friend sitting in her morass of panic and despair.

"Caitlin," she called softly. When the woman didn't respond, Amanda slipped down on the floor beside her and called again. "Baby, come on, look at me."

Caitlin lifted a tear-streaked face to her friend. "Why are we doing this? Why don't I just give up and let them have it? We'll never find that damned deed." She took a deep breath. "And if I have no family left, no one to pass it on to, why do I bother, anyway?"

Amanda gathered her in her arms. Immediately, Caitlin buried her face in Amanda's shoulder. For a few minutes, Amanda just stroked her head, running a comforting hand over and over the fiery waves. Finally, she started to talk, very softly. "Sweetheart, you are a lovely, warm, intelligent, loving woman who has more friends than you realize. You bring a piece of history and heritage to Charleston and to the country with Hobcaw, and your friends are bound and determined to make sure that Pinkney and his pitiful little plan for a yacht club will NOT come to fruition. So know, deed or not, those of us who love you are here for you and are gonna make sure your family's legacy lives on – intact."

Caitlin gave a watery little chuckle. "Sometimes I forget, and that mess with my mother hasn't made things any better. I just felt so... alone and..."

Amanda pulled her a little closer, whispering, "You're very much not alone."

Just then, the phone rang. Caitlin started to move to go pick it up, but Amanda held her. "Let it ring. If it's urgent, you can call back."

The answering machine picked up, and they listened in disbelief as they heard the voice of Caitlin's mother. "Caitlin, dear. I forgive you for your little tantrum the other day. There is a cocktail party at the Russell House on Saturday night. I'll pick you up at 7:00. Please be ready."

Caitlin pulled away from Amanda and walked over to the phone. She stared at it as if it were a venomous snake, rather than a neutral piece of technology, then slowly picked it up and hit speed dial to return the call.

"Hello, Caitlin. Thanks for—"

Caitlin cut her off. "I will not be joining you. I already have plans for Saturday night."

"But daughter, this is a—"

"Mother, no. I will NOT be joining you." With that, she terminated the call. She stood there, gripping the phone tightly, breathing heavily, trying to control her anger. She failed. With a sudden movement, she threw the phone away.

It wasn't a simple toss. Caitlin put her whole body behind the pitch. The phone went sailing across the room, straight into one of the book cases beside the fireplace – one that they had emptied the shelves of over the past couple of weeks. The phone hit the back of the book case – hard.

They both heard it. The wood at the back of the bookcase cracked from the impact. The sound was a very hollow thud.

The two women looked at one another, startled, shocked, and bewildered. A solid book case should not have made a sound like that.

Amanda walked over to inspect the crack. There was a space behind the panel, but how to get into it without destroying the book case was beyond her for the moment. She turned to Caitlin and asked, "Do you have any wood working tools?"

"I have a hammer, a couple of screw drivers, and a pair of pliers. Anything beyond that and I get a handyman to come in."

"I have some tools at my apartment. I can bring them over in the morning. We'll find out what is behind this panel, and I'll do what I can to repair it."

"Thank you." Caitlin looked at Amanda, who was carefully inspecting the woodwork. In a soft voice, she said, "I don't know how I would have gotten through these weeks without you."

In the corner of the room, Siobhan breathed a sigh of relief. "Finally! They have a clue. Perhaps we'll get this little mess resolved soon."

CHAPTER 9

THE REST OF FRIDAY NIGHT HAD GONE BY QUIETLY. The two women talked – well, Caitlin talked and Amanda listened as the young woman vented all of the pain and anger and frustration and loneliness that had plagued her since that first night when Pinkney's paperwork had shown up and her mother had made an ass of herself at the Historical Society building.

Finally, she started talking about the evening they had experienced. "I swear, my mother's ability to deny reality is going to drive me insane. How could she not have gotten the message when she popped in on us the other day?"

"If I'd known, I would have taken you in my arms and kissed you senseless just to send a message." In her mind, Amanda mumbled, 'I'd like to kiss you senseless anyway.'

"Oh, wouldn't that have been a mess!" Caitlin giggled. "We probably would have had to call 911 to handle her stroke."

"Well, look at it this way, if she had a stroke, she wouldn't bother you for a while."

"Oh no, that would be worse. She would expect me to stop working, move home, and take care of her. And with my mother, it would take three or four times longer than the doctors projected for her to recover – she can linger with the best of them."

Amanda shook her head. At least her mother had gotten a clue, even though she had simply switched to trying to hook her up with eligible women – some of whom were utter disasters.

"Would your mother really stroke out if we were together?"

"For starters, you're a woman. Then there's the fact that you're a Yankee. Finally, not only are you a Yankee, you're descended from the single most hated man in the old South. I don't know if she'd stroke out or explode."

Amanda smiled, then softly asked, "Would it stop you?"

Caitlin shifted to look into the eyes of the woman who had her arm around her shoulders. She looked into Amanda's warm brown eyes, seeing a hopeful look there. She thought about how Amanda had quietly stood up for her when she needed it, how she had helped her beyond what most friends would do, had simply been there when she needed someone since the day they'd met. "No, Amanda. It won't stop me." She confirmed her statement with a soft kiss to Amanda's lips. "It won't even slow me down."

Amanda stayed that night – again not as a lover, but as a security blanket and body pillow. She privately wondered how long her sense of honor would be able to hold out against her libido if she had to do this more frequently.

THEY HAD STAYED up late the night before, finally just talking quietly or enjoying the sense of peace being together seemed to bring them, so Amanda slept in – until a painfully bright light broke through the slats of the plantation blinds in Caitlin's room. She looked over at the mop of red hair lying across her shoulder and sighed. It was partially a happy sigh, partially a long suffering one.

She carefully untangled herself from the still sleeping Caitlin, knowing she must have been exhausted after last night's emotional breakdown. She quietly pulled on her shorts and tiptoed down to the kitchen, with a silent mantra repeating in her mind. 'Coffee. Coffee. Coffee.' She knew her way around Caitlin's kitchen pretty well by now, so not only did she put on a pot of coffee, she also pulled together the makings for breakfast. She put on a pot of grits, and while they were cooking, crisped some bacon, grated cheese to go in the grits, and whipped eggs to scramble when Caitlin emerged.

And emerge she did – with tousled hair, a wrinkled t-shirt, bare feet, and a smile that was competing with the sun for brightness – just as Amanda was laying the strips of crisp bacon on a plate covered with a folded paper towel to drain.

"Coffee?"

"Oh, please. Smells wonderful."

"Hope so. I've learned how to properly cook grits for you."

Caitlin grinned. No Charleston breakfast was complete without grits. "Who taught you?"

"I got my landlady to show me. Milk makes a difference – and stirring regularly; I learned the hard way."

Caitlin laughed. "Made a pot or two of hockey pucks, did you?"

Amanda just grinned, popped a couple of pieces of bread in the toaster, dropped a pat of butter in a skillet, and poured in the eggs, gently stirring them. As the eggs cooked, she stirred the cheese into the grits.

Within a couple of minutes, she was serving up scrambled eggs, bacon, grits, and toast. She set both plates on the kitchen table and got herself another cup of coffee. She sat down and watched Caitlin a little nervously, hoping the breakfast would meet with approval. After the first bite of eggs and grits went down Caitlin's maw, a huge grin broke over her' face.

"Okay, you're now officially an honorary Southerner. You passed the biggest test – proper cheesy grits."

Amanda grinned. The two women hadn't eaten dinner last night with all the other issues before them, and both were hungry.

When they finished, Amanda went into the library to examine the shelves in the daylight. She and Caitlin cleared everything off the shelves, then Amanda started to carefully examine every inch of the bookcase. It appeared that there was another set of narrow shelves behind the partition. It also appeared that the bookcase had been fitted together by an expert joiner. There were no nails, didn't appear to be any glue, and very few pegs. The shelves themselves were slotted into the upright panels using a dado joint; the builder had carefully routed out the uprights to hold the shelves securely, and to carry a fair bit of weight. To get the shelves out of the way, she would have to remove the facings.

She carefully examined the facings, looking for any indication of an easy way to remove them. They were joined to the uprights using a tongue and groove joint – one that was solid enough to not require any dowels or glue.

Finally, she carefully examined the back panel, looking for any way to easily remove it. What she found was interesting. The panel was not a single piece of wood; instead, it was made from several panels that ran from side to side of the bookcase, looking solid because the joints were under the shelves. Clearly, this set of shelves was designed to allow relatively easy removal of the facings, and to allow at least some of the shelves to slide out easily. She had found the hidey hole that every old house had.

The problem was the wood hadn't been touched except to dust and polish it for at least 150 years. How to pry the shelves apart when the wood had years of normal expansion and contraction was going to be a challenge.

"Hey, Caitlin!" Amanda called. The cooler she could make the room, the easier it would be to pull the facings off. Caitlin appeared at the door. "Does the house have serious air conditioning?"

"Sure. I had it checked this spring."

"Good, 'cause we need to make this room as cold as possible."

"I have a window unit we could put in here too, if you need it."

"Good idea. Lead on!"

They rather quickly installed the window unit and overrode the thermostat in it to just keep pumping cold air into the room. At the same time, Caitlin turned her first floor thermostat for the house system as low as it would go.

"Okay. I'm gonna go get my tools. I'll be back in a while."

"I'll be waiting. Should I do anything while you're gone?"

Amanda grinned. "Well, you might want to put on a few more clothes."

IT WAS a few minutes after ten when Amanda returned with her wood working tools in a good-sized case beside her. As she drove up to Caitlin's, she noticed a silver Mercedes parked in the driveway behind Caitlin's car. It didn't take a rocket scientist to figure out that Harriet had come to badger her daughter about whatever it was she wanted Caitlin to attend with her that evening.

An evil grin graced Amanda's face as she pulled in beside the silver car, being careful not to block her in.

She pulled out her bag of tools and walked into the kitchen without knocking. She could hear both women's voices coming from the front parlor. She assumed they were there since the library was currently a four-star mess.

Quietly, she walked into the library and dropped her bag. She then walked toward the parlor, calling loudly, "Honey, I'm back." She swept into the parlor, walked over to Caitlin, pulled her into a gentle hug, and laid a tender kiss on very surprised lips.

"Hi, love," gasped Caitlin.

In front of them, Harriet began a string of

incomprehensive blustering sounds, which ended with, "On my soul, how dare you corrupt my daughter this way!"

"She didn't corrupt me. As a matter of fact, I may have corrupted her. I've introduced her to low-country cooking and she's a true convert." Caitlin laughed, her eyes twinkling with humor at the thought of what her mother must be going through. "I told you in clear one and two syllable words that I'm gay. I've been telling you that for years. What's it going to take for you to believe me?"

"Mrs. Balle, I'm sorry if I offended you. I didn't realize you were here."

"Well, you should have. My car is in the driveway – where did you expect me to be?" Harriet was seriously offended by Amanda's evident lack of what she considered common sense. Her face was an interesting shade of red and it was clear she was in a major huff.

"I was in a hurry to get back to Caitlin, so I wasn't really thinking. Please accept my apology."

Caitlin had turned and buried her face in Amanda's shoulder, mostly so she could muffle the laughter that threatened to break out into resounding guffaws.

Harriet glared at Caitlin. "Fine. I understand. I will not expect you to attend any more events with me. If you wish to go to something, let me know." With that, she flounced out of the room and slammed the front door behind her.

Through uncontrolled giggles, Caitlin managed to gasp, "Oh, Amanda – that was priceless!"

Amanda carefully pulled the framing off the bookcase, surprised when it came away from the side panels easily. The woodworker who created these shelves knew what he was doing. He'd created a tongue and groove joint that was secure but not so tight as to make it difficult to remove. As soon as Amanda pulled a shelf out of the dado slot, the back panel dropped down, revealing a five-inch-deep shelf behind it.

Amanda and Caitlin looked into the pocket shelf eagerly. Inside was an old leather folder. They looked at each other, nodding in eager anticipation.

Reverently, Caitlin lifted the portfolio out of its hiding place.

She laid it on the desk and pulled on a pair of cotton document-handling gloves. With a clean cotton cloth, she wiped the dust off the leather, then untied the silk cord that bound the folder closed. She drew in a deep breath, hoping, but almost afraid to be wrong.

In a soft voice, Amanda said, "Open it. You know it's the deed."

Very slowly, Caitlin did just that. There in the leather that had protected it for so many years lay two pieces of parchment, one on each side of the folder. One was a hand-written document, the other a map that clearly showed the Wando River, a much wider Hobcaw Creek, a much larger harbor area, and clearly marked the outline of the property known as Hobcaw Plantation, which stretched from the river to where the creek branched into two channels. The signatures on both the deed and the map included Samuel Balle and Thomas Smith, Landgrave. They were also both witnessed by Robert Gibbes, Landgrave, and Holland

Axtell, Landgrave. The date on both documents was October 18, 1684.

Caitlin reverently closed the leather portfolio. She looked into Amanda's eyes with wonder and relief. "It's real. You found it. Oh, God. Thank you so much." Tears ran down her cheeks; the stress of the search had been more than even she realized.

Amanda took her in her arms and simply held her. It was all she could do. After a few minutes, she gently led Caitlin to the sofa and sat her down. When she tried to extract herself from the arms clinging to her, thinking to retrieve some tissues and a glass of water, she found that Caitlin's' arms were not letting go.

"Stay. Please stay."

"I was just going to get you some tissues and a glass of water."

"I need them, but I need you here more."

"Well, Cait, I'm here whenever you need me."

AMANDA REPAIRED the crack that Caitlin created when she flung the phone into the bookcase, then carefully fitted the pieces of the shelf back together. She went to her apartment late that afternoon to shower and dress for the evening she had planned for Caitlin – an evening that was now even more appropriate as they needed to celebrate.

Promptly at 7:00, Amanda pulled up in front of Caitlin's house. Her Jeep had been cleaned and waxed, with the interior as fresh as it could be made. She got out and went to the door, knocked and waited for Caitlin to come to her. As the door opened, Amanda offered Caitlin a single lavender rose. She had to remember to breathe as she looked at the lovely red-head.

Caitlin had dressed carefully, in a deep blue silk dress with an off the shoulder neckline and flowing skirt. Her hair was pulled back in a French twist, and clear blue aquamarines sparkled in her ears and around her neck, bringing out the blue-green color of her eyes. To Amanda, she was simply magnificent.

Caitlin was just as enthralled by her date's appearance. Amanda, with Sarah's assistance, had found a light gray suit made of raw silk that looked almost silver in the soft light of dusk. The suit was flowing, with a collarless, unstructured jacket and softly fitted trousers. Her elegant image was set off with a shawl collared silk blouse in exactly the same color as the rose she still held in her extended hand.

The two women looked at each another for a long moment, until Amanda shook herself, Caitlin took her rose, and the two closed and locked the door. Amanda helped Caitlin into the car, then whipped around to the driver's side and slid in.

She finally remembered how to talk as she started the car. "I've made a reservation for us at what I now realize is probably the most appropriate restaurant in Charleston for tonight's celebration." Amanda smiled, extremely pleased with her choice from the suggestions Sarah had made.

"Oh? Which one?"

"Circa 1886. I ordered the tasting menu for us. I hoped being able to sample a bunch of their menu items would please you, and it means we won't have to make any choices – we'll get a little of everything!"

"Oh, that sounds like fun." She paused. "But isn't it awfully expensive?"

"It's not that expensive, and I wanted our first real date to be memorable." Amanda grinned. "You have certainly fulfilled that wish of mine. You look absolutely beautiful – well, you always look beautiful, but tonight you look fantastic. You been checking out my fantasies?"

Caitlin blushed, and laid her hand just above her date's knee. "No, I just wanted to look really good tonight."

"You succeeded."

"You look pretty good yourself."

Amanda ducked her head a little, trying to focus on the streets they were driving through instead of looking at the beauty sitting beside her.

They arrived at the restaurant and Amanda handed the car over to the valet. The two were escorted to one of the candle-lit, semi-private alcoves around the edge of the main dining room, which was set with Lenox crystal, white linen, and classic Wedgwood.

An impeccably dressed sommelier approached, carrying a bottle of Veuve Clicquot, which he opened and served in lovely flutes to the two women. "Tonight, your tasting menu will provide three courses, with tasting servings from each of our four thematic menus for each course. These will represent the tastes of native tribes, influences from Europe, flavors brought from Africa, and the fusion of those three that represents South Carolina today. We have selected wines appropriate to each course to complement the menu. I hope you enjoy your evening, ladies."

The tasting menu was spectacular, with everything ranging from peanut soup and foie gras to venison and sea scallops. The desserts were wonderful, and included spiced pear cake, chocolate and berries, a milk tart and an apple souffle. It was all washed down with three very unique and delicious wines, followed by cups of café au lait.

When they were done, they thanked their servers and walked out.

"How did you do that?"

"I paid for the tasting menu in advance, and as we left, I told the maître d' what percentage of tip to add." Amanda grinned, feeling very pleased with herself.

The valet brought the Jeep around and they set off to what was obviously a second destination.

They pulled into the parking lot across from the Republic and again, Amanda came around to help Caitlin out of the vehicle. "I figured dinner and dancing was the right thing for a spectacular first date," she commented, though a grin that would make the Cheshire cat jealous consumed her face.

And it was.

Caitlin found that having Amanda in her arms as they moved to the excellent dance music the disc jockey was spinning was glorious. They both chose to drink spritzers, more for the fluid than the alcohol, and stayed until the bar closed, since they could sleep in on Sunday morning.

Laughing, though tired, they climbed into the Jeep and headed south to Caitlin's house.

"Can we do this again?" asked Caitlin. "I haven't been dancing in a coon's age, and I loved being able to dance with you."

"I'm sure that can be arranged."

"Soon?"

"Very soon."

"Good."

They drove along quietly until they were within a couple of blocks of Caitlin's house.

"Will you stay with me tonight?"

"I can't think of any place I'd rather be, honey."

IT WAS midnight when Pinkney pulled up beside the trailer at Hobcaw. He hadn't driven his distinctive Cadillac, and he definitely didn't want anyone to see him tonight, but he had to look. He was trying to figure out where in the mud flat he would find the Confederate gold – if it was still there at all.

Samuel was sitting on his stone, surveying his world, when Pinkney drove up. In his mind's eye, he could see the ghostly shadows of the buildings, docks and ships that had once graced this beautiful spot. He concentrated his mind to see the night of the burning to see where the Confederate ship went down. Once he had rid his little world of that obnoxious nyaff who started this mess in the first place. He could see why his wife had made a cuckhold of him. No woman in her right head would wish to bed him, Samuel thought.

'Ah, the bloody arse himself,' thought Samuel. 'I shall give him a go for intruding where he's nae welcome.'

He called Tiernan to him. "Go and see to it that the jobber o'er yonder has a difficult night, and let Ronan know that his little mud diggers need to complicate the path."

Tiernan grinned and set off to lay a trap or two. Making

life complicated for the living was almost as good as a jug of whisky.

He then called the banshee. She descended from her tree, eyes glowing red in the night and her ragged gray cloak flapping in the soft evening breeze. "Aye, Laird. Can I, please?"

"Do your best, fair lady."

"I shall. I certainly shall."

Pinkney pulled on a pair of rubber boots and retrieved a flashlight and a six-foot steel pole from the trunk of the car. He slowly walked toward the mud flats, watching his step carefully. Easing out onto the flats, he started poking into the mud with his pole, trying to find something – anything under the reddish-brown mud. After two steps, his pole hit something about six inches under the mud. A rather irate mud skipper popped up, following the path the pole had made, flinging mud into Pinkney's face with his franticly flipping fins and tail.

"Fucking fish!" Pinkney cursed.

He stepped around the flopping fish and moved forward a few cautious steps. The fish followed him, flipping more mud on him. For a few more feet, he found nothing, but the next step he took was right over one of the tunnels that the mud skippers had created. His foot sank into the mud past his knee, immediately filling his boot with mud. He tried to gain some traction by using his pole to reach for a firm bottom. Instead, the pole sank into more mud. Finally, he realized he was going to have to lie down in the mud to be able to pull his leg and foot free of the mud filled boot. He carefully lay back, sitting his flashlight in the mud beside him so he would have his hands free to help pull his foot free. He didn't notice it sinking into the soft mud until the light went out.

Finally, he pulled himself free. He was covered in mud, his flashlight was gone, and he'd strained his ankle freeing it from the mud-lined boot.

He stood up and slowly started back toward his car. A pair of glowing eyes appeared in front of him. The creature's head was tilted to one side, looking at him curiously. The creature lunged at Pinkney, aiming for his right hand.

Pinkney screamed, yanking his hand away from the raccoon. His fear of rabies was running on high. He floundered through the mud to dry land as quickly as he could – which was, unfortunately, not very quickly. The 'coon managed to nip at his shirt and pull off his wrist watch before he squished his way to dry land.

That wasn't the end of his problems, though. Tiernan scattered a lovely trail of sandspurs in his path. They wouldn't have been so bad if he had his shoes on, but they stuck into the soft skin in the arch of his foot like having a hundred little needles stuck into his foot at the same time. Actually, he did have a hundred little needles stuck into his foot.

Cursing, Pinkney hopped on one foot, trying to pluck the irritating burrs out of the other. It was a shame his balance was so poor. Tiernan managed to drop him butt first into the sandspur patch with just a slight puff of wind – well, maybe a little more than a SLIGHT puff of wind.

As Pinkney howled, a new sound joined him. It started low, just enough to notice, but quickly rose in both volume and pitch until it sounded like some sort of emergency siren. Not the kind that ambulances or fire trucks used, but the kind that kept going and going, warning of an impending tornado. Except it wasn't a siren. It was a woman's voice, raised in soul rending grief.

Desperate to find the source of that sound that was making his spine shiver and his bowels contract, Pinkney looked around, searching for but not finding the source of that sound; the wailing kept rising in both pitch and volume. Finally, his frantic searching found the source of the terrible sound. Apparently floating in front of the great live oak tree beside the cemetery was the figure of a woman with long, flowing white blond hair, what looked like a beautiful figure clothed in flowing gray robes, but with glaring red eyes, a figure whose mouth was open in a terribly shriek. As he watched, the woman seemed to age before his eyes, transforming from a beautiful woman in her prime to a mummified corpse. Yet the shrieking continued.

Pinkney's bowels let go.

He leapt to his feet, ignoring the pain of the sandspurs, and ran for his car.

As the car roared down the road, flinging crushed oyster shells and dust behind him, Tiernan, Ciara, and Samuel joined together at the stone, laughing at the fleeing man.

THE TWO WOMEN were quiet during the last few blocks of the drive to Caitlin's house.

Caitlin was tired but finally felt like her life was falling back into something that was working. She had found the deed, she had told her mother off, her work was going reasonably well despite the other stresses, she had made new friends, and Amanda – well, what was growing with Amanda was something very special.

Amanda was feeling very pleased with herself. Their first official date had gone very well, with the pleasure on Caitlin's face with their wonderful dinner giving her a warm glow. The memory of having Caitlin in her arms dancing sensuously in a charming environment and without the grungy décor of most gay bars was wonderful. And now Caitlin wanted her to stay. Every time she had stayed in the past had been because Caitlin needed companionship and comfort due to the stress of her circumstances and the intense loneliness she felt as a result of her mother's manipulations. Amanda hoped that maybe tonight would be different. Her libido agreed – vehemently.

She pulled into Caitlin's driveway and parked by the kitchen door. Before she cut off the engine, she turned to Caitlin. "I was hoping you'd ask me to stay, so I brought a change of clothes. I hope I wasn't being too presumptuous."

Caitlin smiled. "You weren't being presumptuous. You were being hopeful. Come on in; we can have a cup of tea, unwind a little, and then see what happens."

Amanda cut the engine, reached behind the seat, and grabbed a small overnight bag, then leapt out of the car to open the door for Caitlin.

Caitlin found she enjoyed this little piece of formality between them. Of course, she was capable of getting out of the car by herself. There was something in the caring that the moment of old-fashioned courtesy conveyed that made her feel special.

They went into the kitchen, and Caitlin flipped on the

light, then turned on the heat under the kettle. "What flavor tea for you, dear?"

"Um, whatever you're having," Amanda mumbled as she set her bag on one of the kitchen chairs. She was looking at Caitlin and not seeing or thinking of much else.

Caitlin pulled a couple of mugs from the cabinet, dropped a couple of sleepy time bags into them, and added a spoon of honey to Amanda's cup. She turned and looked at her, seeing nothing but tenderness and a gentle wanting in her soft brown eyes.

She walked the few steps to stand in front of Amanda and took her face between her hands, saying very softly, "This was the loveliest evening I can ever remember having. The dinner was good, the dancing was wonderful, but the best thing about it is the company."

She tenderly kissed Amanda's soft lips, savoring the sweetness of the moment. Her hands dropped to Amanda's shoulders, drawing her closer.

Amanda had the good sense to slide her hands around Caitlin's waist, pulling her even closer as the kiss evolved from tender thanks to gentle exploration. Just as the intensity was about to go yet another step higher, the kettle whistled, startling both of them.

They separated, both laughing a little, and Caitlin poured hot water into each of their mugs, then set them at the kitchen table.

"I guess we should talk."

Amanda grinned. "Probably. We seem to have spent the summer evolving into..."

"What?"

"Exactly. Evolving into what?"

Caitlin blushed. "Certainly, into friends."

Amanda took Caitlin's hands into hers. "Yes, friends, and I hope good friends." She waited for Caitlin to add to her statement.

"And I think we've moved into something more."

"If that kiss was any indication, I'd say we're looking at more than just friends – and to be honest, I'd like even more, if you're willing. I care for you a great deal." Amanda's last words were said very softly.

Caitlin dropped her head to stare into her now cooling tea. "I would too," she whispered.

"Do I hear a '"but"' in your voice?" Amanda could feel her heart constricting in her chest, scared of what was coming.

Caitlin took a deep breath. "I care for you as well. You have been nothing but wonderful to me since the day we met. I worry, though. I know you're just here for this job, and I'm afraid to let myself get too involved, for fear you'll leave and I'll be alone again..."

"Shhhhh, sweetheart." Amanda took a deep breath. Caitlin's fear was real and she'd been honest about wanting a long-term relationship and building a family at one point. "My contract isn't just for Hobcaw Point. It's three years for Charleston County – that means multiple projects. With the people I'm meeting, I'm sure I can find more work when the contract is up. I love Charleston." She bent her head and pulled Caitlin's hands up so she could gently kiss her knuckles. "I'd love to settle down here, and I hope I have a chance to settle down with you."

Caitlin looked into those warm brown eyes and saw a possibility for the future. For the first time, she believed in the possibility, after years of expecting to spend her life alone.

Amanda got up and went over to kneel beside Caitlin. She simply took her in her arms, gently holding her without any other demands, quietly waiting for Caitlin.

HARRIET BALLE WAS NOT ACCUSTOMED to arising early. Where other people found the crisp quality of early morning refreshing, Harriet thought dew was just an annoyance designed to make her dressing gown damp around the hem when she walked through the grass to get the paper. She wandered into the kitchen, found the French press, boiled some water, and made herself a pot of chicory coffee she had sent from New Orleans to meet her demanding taste.

She sat down and immediately opened the paper to the society page. She read the brief report about last night's event – the one she had wanted to take her daughter to in order to meet eligible men from the right families. She sighed.

"That damned Yankee has turned her head. What do I do to get Caitlin to realize that this is not the right path for her? I know; I'll talk to David Gibbs. As a commissioner, he can get rid of her. If I send her on her way, then I'll be able to get Caitlin back on track."

She finished her cup of coffee, then poured herself another, staring at the clock as she did so. She couldn't call David before ten in the morning on a Sunday morning. In fact, she had never called him at home before, even though she'd had the number for years. 'Well, this is an emergency,' she thought.

HENRY PINKNEY WALKED out of the 24-hour emergency care facility, grimacing at the pain of walking, and not anticipating sitting down in the car with relish. The extensive population of sandspurs embedded in his foot and backside had required he do something more drastic than just plucking them out himself. Some of them he couldn't even reach, so he walked into the emergency care facility, gave them a false name, and paid cash to have his foot and ass tended to by a nurse practitioner who had a hell of a time not laughing out loud.

A quick trip to the local Walmart got him clean clothes, a stop in a no-tell motel got him a shower, and a run through a car wash and detailing shop removed the hellish pile of mud he'd left in the driver's seat. His muddy and shit stained clothes went into the trash.

When asked how he came to be perforated by hundreds of sandspurs, he answered very shortly, "I went gigging and slipped." After all, he was – he just wasn't gigging for frogs; he was gigging for gold.

He was home before Sherry was out of bed. He hurriedly dressed in his own clothes, then left to return to Hobcaw to make sure no one discovered evidence of his evening foray.

CAITLIN WOKE when the sun managed to invade her room with glaring late summer light. She looked at the clock. It was only about eight o'clock. She was incredibly comfortable, held snugly against Amanda's warm body. She thought about going back to sleep, since they had stayed up until very late in the night, cuddling and talking, working through both of their insecurities about getting into a real relationship, until they finally realized that, except for one thing, they were already in a real, and gently romantic, relationship.

Caitlin knew how Amanda made her feel every time she touched her, held her, gently kissed her. She felt each touch in her heart, in the shivers they sent up her spine, and if she was being truthful with herself, deep in her gut and between her legs. Yup. Amanda turned her on as well as giving her a sense of safety, of warmth, of completion. Yup. She was falling, and falling seriously, for the sandy haired, brown eyed, sun-kissed, sexy as hell, gentle as a lamb engineer.

She slipped her hand under the t-shirt that Amanda had worn to sleep in, running her fingertips lightly over the firm stomach, then up to the solid rib cage and gently around the edge of soft breasts. The body under her hand drew in a sharp breath, and Caitlin looked up into a pair of shining, warm brown eyes.

"Need improved access?" Amanda smiled as she slightly arched her back, offering herself to Caitlin's questing fingers.

When Caitlin shyly nodded, Amanda sat up and quickly stripped off her shirt, taking a moment to gently kiss her. "There you go. Help yourself." As she lay back down, she slid her own hand under Caitlin's t-shirt, running the palm of her hand up and down her back, soothing and caressing soft skin, and slowly moving down toward the soft skin of her buttocks.

Caitlin eased up on one arm, looking down at the half-naked form beneath her own. The skin where the sun had not browned it was fair, almost milky. The breasts were firm, with nipples that had tightened so much they looked almost painful. In fact, Amanda was, to Caitlin's mind, beautiful, sexy, and perfect. Fingers explored everywhere, followed by gently exploring lips until Amanda arched when Caitlin took a nipple into her mouth and suckled.

At the same time, Amanda's hand tightened on Caitlin's butt, pulling her as close as she could. Panting a bit, Amanda observed, "We both seem to be overdressed – you more than me."

Caitlin pulled back, stripped off her t-shirt and panties, and yanked Amanda's shorts down abruptly – and with a little help from Amanda's raised hips.

She turned back to the still reclining Amanda, with both looking appreciatively for a moment before Caitlin laid the length of her body against the woman beneath her. Their legs intertwined and their nipples met, drawing groans from both of them, before their bodies joined completely. The feel of skin on skin, the pressure of thighs in critical places, the sensual impact of belly to belly and breast to breast was enough to push both of them up and over the edge. That was just the beginning of a morning of joyous exploration.

Siobhan, who had decided to check on her grandchild, was down in the library. She heard them and smiled. 'About damned time you bedded her, child.'

CHAPTER 10

PROMPTLY AT TEN O'CLOCK, HARRIET BALLE called David Gibbs's home number. She was surprised when a man whose voice sounded familiar but wasn't Commissioner Gibbs answered the phone.

"May I speak with David Gibbs, please? It's Harriet Balle calling."

"Oh, hello, Harriet. It's Spencer Rowe. Let me get David for you."

As she waited for Gibbs to come to the phone, she wondered briefly about her daughter's attorney having answered the phone. 'I suppose they're friends having brunch together,' she speculated.

"Mrs. Balle, it's David Gibbs. How can I help you?"

"Good morning, Mr. Gibbs. Ah, I have a rather delicate issue that I thought you might be able to help me with."

"If it is something I can do..." Harriet Balle was one of the worst brown nosers he knew – and anything she was asking for would undoubtedly be about maintaining the social snobbery she so loved.

"Well, it's rather sensitive, but you are such an understanding gentleman, I hope you can appreciate my position."

"Go on, Mrs. Balle."

"You know my daughter, Caitlin, I think."

"Yes, I know Dr. Balle. We've met through my work with the Historical Commission."

Harriet took a deep breath. "It seems my daughter has formed an, um, unfortunate relationship with that engineer you have working at Hobcaw. I'm appalled that she's been drawn into such an unnatural attraction – and to a descendant of that dreadful general Sherman too."

"What makes Caitlin being friends with Ms. Sherman a problem, Mrs. Balle?" He thought to himself, 'Great. One more version of bigotry that poor Cait has to deal with.'

Harriet was offended, and her rising pitch and volume illustrated that. "Why, Mr. Gibbs, it's unnatural, that's why. Not only is it a totally inappropriate relationship between Caitlin and someone who is simply not of the same class, but it's two women. TWO WOMEN. Caitlin should marry a good Southern man and have children to carry on the Balle heritage."

"Again, what is it you want me to do?"

"Why, that's obvious. Fire that Sherman woman on the grounds of moral depravity! That woman has seduced my daughter!"

"I'm afraid there is nothing I can do, Mrs. Balle."

"Why not? You're a commissioner!"

"That's exactly why, ma'am. First, Caitlin is an adult. She is free to associate with whomever she wishes. Second, and I can't be any clearer about this, I cannot ask for Ms. Sherman to be terminated because of her preference. That is her choice and any action against her would result in a very nasty lawsuit for violation of her civil rights. Third, if Caitlin and Ms. Sherman are friends, and even if they are more than friends, I'm very glad for Caitlin. Amanda Sherman is a charming and very honorable human being, and I'm glad Caitlin has found a good friend." He paused, waiting for the woman on the other end of the line to respond. When the line remained silent, he said, "If there is nothing else, Mrs. Balle, have a good day."

"Damn, damn, DAMN!" Harriet cursed. She paced around her kitchen trying to figure out another way to get rid of the Sherman bitch. "Pinkney – as much as I hate to deal with that little slime, he can be bought."

HENRY WAS surprised when he crawled into the house at around eleven. Sherry usually wasn't up on Sunday morning until about noon, but there she was, sitting at the kitchen table, fully dressed, coiffed and made up, drinking a cup of coffee and looking through the newspaper.

"Oh, so you are alive. I was wondering when you'd show up."

Henry poured himself a cup of coffee – a much needed cup of coffee.

"So, was she good?"

"What are you talking about?"

"Whoever you were with all night. The one you left here after eleven to meet. Was she good?"

"I wasn't with anyone. I went to look at a project, to see how it was coming, and had an accident."

"Sure. I believe you, dear husband, and I believe you will be buying me a new pair of diamond earrings too."

"Certainly, dear," he grumbled. Sherry was an expensive hobby, but she looked good on his arm, which made him look good.

CAITLIN CALLED Spencer around two that afternoon – shortly after she and Amanda had finally gotten up and eaten something.

Spencer was thrilled to hear from her, even on a Sunday. The whole mess with what Pinkney was trying to do had him righteously pissed off, so stopping the little twerp was high on his list of things to do. Then the call that morning from Caitlin's mother had added frosting to his self-righteous cake.

"Hi, honey. How are you? And what is this thing I hear about with you and Amanda Sherman?"

"Hi, Spencer. I'm good. In fact, I'm very good. How are David and Davie?"

"They're fine, though David's pretty pissed at your mother right now."

Caitlin laughed. "He needs to get in line. She's got me to the point where I'm throwing things. What did she do this time?"

"Ah oh. I take it this trouble is nothing new?"

"There's been trouble for years. My mother cannot accept that I'm gay. Any woman I get involved with is an evil influence that has led me down the path of corruption, and all I need is to find and marry a good Southern man and have nice little children of the confederacy."

"Oh, we know. She called David this morning trying to get him to fire Amanda for moral depravity. He read her a riot act about bigotry and violation of civil rights, not to mention that you're an adult and free to make your own decisions."

"Oh, I'll bet that went over with my mother like a..., yeah, well, you get my point."

"She was not happy. So, when do we get to invite you and Amanda over to dinner? I want to get to know this paragon better."

"After I've had a chance to know her better as more than a friend. She's been a good friend throughout this whole mess with Pinkney, I have to say. In fact, she's found something you'll be interested in."

"Oh, really? I know she's been collecting artifacts out at Hobcaw. Did she find something cool?"

"Very cool, but not out at Hobcaw. She found it in my library."

"Oh, my God. She found the deed."

"She did indeed. I'm taking it to Sarah in the morning to have her get someone to authenticate it."

"Good girl. This is fantastic. What's the date on it? I'm really curious."

"1684. And it's signed by three of the original landgraves – one sold the property and the other two witnessed it. It should be easy enough to validate the signatures."

"You have just guaranteed that the property will be put on the Historical Register immediately, and that nothing in Pinkney's claim is valid. I've already killed the idea that Hobcaw is the only place available to provide a critical and necessary county facility and that the property has been abandoned."

"So eminent domain is dead."

"As a doornail."

"Thank you so much, Spencer. It means a lot to me."

"It's what I'm here for, honey." He started to say goodbye, but stopped for a second. "Say hello to Amanda for me. Tata, dear."

Caitlin laughed and hung up. She turned to Amanda. "You have two new fans – Spencer Rowe and his partner, Commissioner David Gibbs."

MONDAY WAS busy for a number of people.

Caitlin took the deed to Sarah to get the appropriate people in line to validate it so the court would have to accept it. After a few phone calls, the document was carefully packaged, still in its leather portfolio, and shipped (with a great deal of insurance) to Harvard for immediate validation.

Spencer provided the court with an update on the status of the deed and the steps being taken to validate the document.

Amanda revised the documentation and plats to demonstrate how more economic and usable the Wando River site would be for the yacht club, to meet a request from David Gibbs.

Judge Monk tried to call Pinkney to arrange an immediate meeting. He couldn't find him.

Harriet tried to reach Pinkney, though she was just as successful as Monk had been.

The Historical Commission submitted their recommendation that Hobcaw Point Shipyard be named on the Historical Register with an additional request for rush finalization.

Ronan had his minions collected a few gold coins from the Confederate ship's hoard and placed them at the stern of the ship's remains to misguide the dredging crew.

David Gibbs got together with a number of other commissioners to create a plan for moving the yacht club to the Wando River site and to make an offer to Ms. Balle for the property.

Pinkney realized that things with Sherry were rocky. Something she had said the day before made him suspicious, so he spent his day following her.

By the end of the day, Amanda and Caitlin were both beat – from the residual of lack of sleep over the weekend, the many things they each had had to do during the day, and the inevitable stress that 'hurry up and wait' placed on them. They ordered some bog from the local carry out, settled down in the library, which was partially put back together, and watched an old movie together before sleep claimed both of them.

Siobhan smiled down at the two sleeping women curled up on the big leather sofa. They made such a cute pair. The old woman was very pleased. Now all she had to do was bring Samuel into line. She popped over to her stone, sitting next to the old man, who was watching Ronan and his crew settle things in the mud flats. "Husband, I believe you'll get your heir."

"What mean you, woman?"

"Caitlin has found her mate."

"Oh." He was silent for a while. "The Sherman wench?"

"Yes. And a right proper mate she is. She found your panel."

"Good. Did she put it back together?"

"Aye, that she did, and you canna tell it was opened."

"Good."

FOR AMANDA AND CAITLIN, the week was looking to be fairly quiet – a quiet they both looked forward to eagerly. They were in that crazy first flush of a love affair and all either of them could think about was spending time with each another, preferably very close—in fact, so close that you couldn't pry a piece of paper between their two naked bodies. Work intruding was nothing more or less than a massive annoyance, with Amanda focused on the possibilities of the site over by the river and Caitlin trying, without much success, to put together her display of colonial life.

MONK FOUND Pinkney on Tuesday afternoon. It was not a happy meeting.

"Did you know that Balle found that damned deed? It's old enough, so it's a historical record. It's already gotten so much attention that trying to steal it is impossible."

"Oh, hell."

"Pinkney, you screwed up – big time. What are you gonna do to fix this?"

"Well, I have a special crew lined up to start sucking up the mud over where the ship probably sank starting Friday night after Ms. By-The-Book leaves for the weekend. We'll be sucking mud non-stop until early Monday morning, and sieving the mud to make sure we don't miss anything."

"Good. I guess it's the best we can do."

"I'll keep you posted."

ON THURSDAY, David Gibbs met with the team from the Historical Society to discuss the potential impact of the planned yacht club if they moved the location to the Wando River side of Hobcaw Point, and further the possibility of helping Caitlin Balle turn the shipyard site into some sort of historic attraction for the area.

"You know, some of those foundations out at Hobcaw date back to pre-revolutionary buildings. The Balle's built for durability, and even with the fire damage and the years of exposure, there's still enough there to probably rebuild the site, between what Caitlin's got in records and what's still in the ground." Helen Sothel was an architect in her day-job and the idea of rebuilding excited her. She had also been turned down by Pinkney as the architect for the yacht club.

Nate Wyche, who owned one of the old hotels in town, laughed. "Helen, if you have an opportunity to build something, you will. We don't even know if Dr. Balle has an interest in creating a historic site."

"Well, we all know something like that costs a fortune," Daniel Amy the financier spoke from his own experience in renovating one of the historical homes near the Battery.

"Doesn't she have some money of her own?" Nate asked.

"Her mother has most of it. She won't see it until the old bitch dies, and I don't think she's planning on relieving us of her presence any time soon," groaned Daniel.

David listened to his guests with some amusement. He'd known them all since they were kids and some things never changed. He decided it was time to intervene. "If Caitlin wants to sell the land on the Wando and keep the shipyard property, she'll at least have enough to make a start, and it will still cost the county less than what Pinkney wanted to do."

"Ah, yes, the notorious Mr. Pinkney. I've been doing some poking in his actions as a commissioner. Wish I could say I'd caught him in an outright crime, but he's certainly done some damned stupid things. I'll keep looking. He needs to go away."

Daniel looked thoughtful. "I have a friend who does the county audits. Maybe I'll give him a heads up. Couldn't hurt and might keep Pinkney busy enough so he won't do any more damage."

FRIDAY MORNING WAS BRIGHT, and it was clear it was going to be a hot, muggy day. Amanda groaned as she wandered into the bathroom for a shower. 'Why is the weather here hotter in September than it was in June?' she wondered. She pulled on a pair of khaki walking shorts, a white polo shirt, knee length socks, and hiking boots. Commissioner Gibbs had asked her for a tentative layout if they were to place the yacht club facing the Wando River, and that meant walking the land for her.

Caitlin called up the stairs, "Breakfast is ready – come on before it gets cold."

Amanda thudded down the stairs, eager to stuff her face with the grits and cheese, and sausage and sweet potato hash with a poached egg that she knew Caitlin had fixed for breakfast. When Caitlin realized that Amanda was bad about having lunch and noticed she had lost a little weight as a result, she had started feeding her robust breakfasts whenever she stayed over.

"What's on today's agenda, honey?" Amanda asked as she poured herself a cup of coffee.

"I'm hoping to hear from Harvard about the document so Spencer can finish up this ridiculous court thing. And David Gibbs asked if he could come by with Nate Wyche, so it could be interesting. He suggested Sarah join us if she could."

"I suspect the property's been officially put on the register." Amanda broke the egg yolk over the hash and took a bite. "Damn, woman. This is delicious!"

"How about you?"

"Oh, I get to hike all over the Wando River side and figure out where to put things like docks, a swimming pool, and the main building for the yacht club, not to mention places to lay water, sewer, electric and phone lines."

"In other words, you're going out to play in civil engineer heaven!" Caitlin laughed.

"Hey, at least I'm not trying to figure out how to do all that on top of a site that should be an archeological dig," Amanda defended herself.

"I know, and you've been a saint about protecting the site."

"It needed protecting." Amanda grinned at Caitlin. "So did you. Life wasn't being very nice to you when we met."

"You know, I may be a little weird, but it felt funny not to have Mother calling me about some snobby event she wanted me to attend this week."

"Funny awkward, funny sad, or funny good?"

Caitlin thought about it for a minute while she walked over and sat herself down in Amanda's lap, laying her head on the always available shoulder. "Funny good."

HARRIET BALLE HAD BEEN HEARING all sorts of rumors about her daughter's property at Hobcaw Point. Was the county going to take it? Was it going to be declared a historic site? Was that atrocious little Pinkney going to build a yacht club on it? Whatever was going on, Harriet was sure that sooner or later, Caitlin would come to her senses. All she could do now was wait – and keep her ears open.

She started scanning the social calendar for opportunities to find appropriate men for her daughter.

DAVID GIBBS and Spencer Rowe walked into Caitlin's office promptly at one o'clock, both grinning like Cheshire cats. "Well, lady, I think between the two of us, we can make your day."

"Okay, Spencer – what's the good news?" Caitlin grinned at him, expecting the package he held to hold the deed to her property.

"First, Harvard has confirmed that your deed is authentic." He set the package that held the deed on her desk. "Their report states that 'the binder is clearly in the style of the period between 1660 and 1700, and the dating was verified by carbon dating. The parchment is of a similar date. The ink, iron gall ink, is appropriate to the period. Finally, there were three signatures of historical significance on the document. We have compared all three signatures to known versions and find no serious variations in the signatures. We conclude they are original and are validated as being signatures of the known entities.'"

Caitlin grinned. "Well, not only do we have the deed, we have a document of historical significance."

"You most assuredly do," Sarah Highsmith said from the door, where she had been standing listening to Spencer read the report. "When you finish with the courts, the museum would be pleased if you would let us display it – on loan of course – as part of the colonial exhibit?"

"Of course – it's my exhibit anyway." Caitlin grinned at her friend.

Nate looked at Caitlin. "You have more than just a document that's officially a historical artifact." He reached into his jacket pocket and pulled out an envelope. "Here's the official confirmation that Hobcaw Point Shipyard and the ruins of the buildings on the site are officially on the National Register of Historic Places. The cemetery on the property is included in the register."

"So Pinkney's yacht club is officially dead." Caitlin's grin grew, but then something crossed her mind. "What about Amanda's job? With no yacht club, she'll be out of work."

"Well, two things about that. First, her contract is not specific to the yacht club project – she's the county's civil engineer for the next three years. Second, your deed gives you more than the grounds of the old shipyard. The Balle plantation extended all the way up to the river. There is plenty of land that is not covered by the register restrictions along the riverfront that the county would be happy to purchase for a facility. So it will be up to you – if you're willing to sell the county some land on the river front, Amanda will be on the Hobcaw Point site for a while."

Sarah grinned. "Of course, you could put her to work on the historic site, gentlemen."

"Daniel Amy's looking into finding grant money for that."

"Smart man."

"So, Caitlin, what do you say to us taking you and Amanda out to dinner tonight to celebrate?" Nate grinned. "Come over to the Fox around seven. I'll have the chef make us something special. How many will we have?"

"There's me and Amanda. There's Spencer and David – you bringing your son?"

"I don't think so – this is a grownups thing, dear."

"Sarah?"

"We'll be there."

So Nate planned to feed eight very happy, celebratory

adults. He would make sure that they'd have the best of what The Swamp Fox could offer.

"Let me make a phone call and make sure Amanda can join us."

She hit a speed dial button on her cell phone. It took four rings before Amanda answered. "Hi, baby. What's up?"

"We've been invited out to dinner tonight. Wanna go?"

"Sure. I always like meeting your friends."

"Great. Can you get home early? So we can talk before we go?"

"Of course. I'll stop by my place to pick up some clothes, then come to you. I can shower and dress there and we can talk."

"Sounds perfect. I should be home in about an hour. I'll see you soon."

"You will probably beat me there, but I'll hurry."

"Okay. Later, gator."

Caitlin turned to her friends and grinned. "It will be so much fun to tell her."

PINKNEY HAD BEEN PARKED behind a bush on Molasses Lane, watching for Amanda's Jeep. He figured as soon as she was gone, they could start looking for the gold.

He drove down Hobcaw Drive to the dirt path to the trailer and parked his car behind it so it wouldn't be obvious to a casual passerby. Pulling on a new pair of rubber boots, he hiked down to the harbor area, where he hailed the guys on the dredging barge. One of the crew had been watching for him, and immediately started poling the small, square-nosed flat-bottomed jon boat over to collect him.

Pinkney climbed onto the barge as the silent man tied off the small boat, then joined him. At the rear of the barge, Raymond was sorting through some papers on a clipboard.

"Are we ready?"

"Yup. Tell us where to start sucking."

Pinkney pulled a copy of the old map that Caitlin had found and turned over to the court as part of her proof of ownership – the one that showed the piers from shortly before the Civil War. "The boat would have been moored around here." He indicated an area on the old map. "I think what I'm looking for would have been in the stateroom at the back of the boat."

"All right. The Sherman woman's gone, so we can get started." Raymond motioned for Pinkney to follow him.

Off the stern of the barge was a rack with a fine mesh liner. A small pump was flooding water over the mesh. There was a hose as well to wash the mud away from anything that was brought up. There was a spot light over the rig, so it would be well-lit through the night. "This is your station, Henry. You get to look for whatever it is you expect to find. We'll get started now."

The big diesel engine that ran the suction pump rumbled to life, then began chugging. A foot-wide hose lowered into the mud and started vacuuming it up. After a few minutes, mud started gushing out of the tube at the stern of the barge and Pinkney started washing mud through the mesh, leaving a pile of dead reeds, fish bones, small pebbles, and other swampy detritus.

AMANDA SWUNG into the driveway to her now seldom used apartment in less than an hour after talking with Caitlin. Something was up, she was sure, but going to dinner with Caitlin's friends, and especially going as her girlfriend, was worth rushing around on a Friday afternoon.

She pulled the gray suit and lavender shirt out of the closet along with her dress boots. It was her only fairly dressy date clothing. A hair brush and a mother of pearl hair clip went into her purse and she was off again.

In another ten minutes, she pulled into Caitlin's driveway. The red-head was waiting at the kitchen door, grinning broadly.

"What's the big grin for?" Amanda asked as she pulled her clothes out of the backseat of the Jeep.

"We're going out to celebrate tonight."

Amanda bounced up the couple of steps to the kitchen door, leaned down and kissed the girl, and asked, "What are we celebrating?"

Caitlin shut the kitchen door and went to the fridge to get the limeade pitcher while Amanda dropped her clothes over the back of a chair.

"Well, the deed was validated."

"Fantastic. I assume that will end the mess with Pinkney."

Caitlin poured two glasses of limeade. "The property is officially on the register."

"Even better!" Amanda took a big slug of her limeade.

"And the county wants to buy the Wando River side of the property."

Amanda put down her glass, took the glass out of Caitlin's hand, and embraced her. "Fabulous – you get a chunk of change and the county gets their yacht club on the right piece of land."

"And you get to keep your job."

"I think we should go upstairs and celebrate privately before we go out with your friends."

"I think you have brilliant ideas, oh my so smart engineer."

RONAN LAY under an overhanging tree branch, enjoying the flow of water over his skin and watching the idiots on the barge bungle around trying to suck up the mud flat. They were doing an impressive job of filling the creek with mud – such an impressive job that he and his aquatic friends had absolutely zero visibility under water. He would have to do something about that when the human flesh sacks were done.

He grinned at the assortment of things the big vacuum was sucking up. There were bits of old wood, showing signs of having been charred, odd pieces of metal fittings, a couple of short lengths of hemp rope, a lot of fish bones and vegetation, and an amazing amount of reddish gray mud. Soon they would find the handful of coins he'd scattered in the muck. That should get their attention.

A shadowy figure appeared to his right. "Evening, Samuel."

"Ronan."

"They are making a right proper mess. I wish them well, as they are about thirty feet from their goal."

"They are desperate. Young Caitlin found the deed and her solicitor has done right in all ways. They are even talking about rebuilding the shipyard to show folks how we did it in my day."

"I wish them well. How long until these nyaffs have to pack up their rig?"

"The Sherman woman will be back Monday morning, so I'd say Sunday night late."

"Good. We will be sure they dinna get to the bow by then."

"Excellent. My lady wife will stay with the girls to be sure they are in line."

"Good. Do nae let me keep you, then, sir." Ronan wanted to go back to the quiet luxuriating he had been indulging in before Samuel popped in.

The dredging continued.

Around three in the morning, Pinkney let out a shriek. "Gold – we've got a gold coin. We must be in the right area."

Ronan just snickered.

CHAPTER 11

CAITLIN HAD LUXURIATED IN THE COMBINED pleasure of warm water flowing over her shoulders while Amanda knelt in front of her, holding her hips firmly to keep her upright and using her lips and tongue to amazingly effective purpose, ensuring that even though they were in the shower, she would need to wash various portions of her body again before she could go out. Otherwise, the aroma would be distinctively revealing as to the nature of their relationship. Her hands tightened in Amanda's hair as her hips bucked, and a low moan rose in both pitch and volume as her body reached its pinnacle and tumbled over into the abyss.

Amanda slid to her feet, holding Caitlin upright, gently kissing the woman who had the muscle tension of a wet noodle, and feeling very pleased with herself and the impact she had on Caitlin. She murmured loving nonsense in Caitlin's ear until the waterlogged red-head regained control of her limbs and sense of balance.

"You okay, sweetie?"

"Umm. Very okay, thank you." Caitlin kissed Amanda's neck, still holding on as the water fell over both of them.

"I think we need to get out soon, baby," Amanda said, her voice conveying her reluctance to do so.

"Why? It's nice right here," Caitlin whispered.

"One, we're running out of hot water."

"Oh, but you keep me so warm."

"And two, we have to get dressed and go to dinner with your friends."

"Oh." It was a very disappointed sound.

DINNER THAT EVENING WAS DELIGHTFUL. The staff had set up one of the smaller banquet rooms for their boss's dinner. Nate Wyche had given his chef free rein to produce whatever he felt like for a festive dinner for eight. When the guests arrived, they were escorted to the room by the maître d'. There, they were greeted by a grinning Nate and his wife Georgia.

Nate gave Caitlin a hug, then turned to shake hands with Amanda. "Miss Sherman, you look lovely tonight. Let me introduce you to my wife, Georgia." He turned to look at the other people in the room. "I believe you know everyone else here tonight."

"Good evening, Mr. Wyche. A pleasure to meet you, Mrs. Wyche. Please, call me Amanda."

"Georgia, Amanda has been contracted as Charleston County's official civil engineer, and so far, I understand she's been doing an excellent job."

"I'm pleased to meet you, Amanda – and call me Georgia. I'm avoiding Mrs. Wyche as much as I avoid my mother-in-law."

"Aww, sweetie, she's not that bad." Nate paused for a moment. "Now that I think of it, yes, she is." They all laughed.

Spencer Rowe and David Gibbs strolled up, having heard the exchange about mothers-in-law. David grumbled, "Poor Caitlin's got us beat in the overbearing mother department."

"Oh, hell. What did she do now?" Amanda's protective instincts were on full alert.

"She called me to try and get you fired because you two are friends."

Amanda's head dropped until her chin was resting on her chest. Caitlin had mentioned something about her mother trying to stir up more trouble, but hadn't been specific.

David grinned. "Yup. I read her a riot act on civil rights, contract law, and outright bigotry." He looked at Amanda. "Your contract is safe."

Amanda let out a breath she hadn't realized she was holding. "Yes, well, thank you, David. Mrs. Balle and I have had a couple of, um, interesting run-ins."

"Well, you've impressed the entire council, if you don't count Pinkney and his obsession with the shipyard area, with your thoughtful recommendations about the yacht club. I'm sure there are other projects around the county that could use your professional attention as well, so we would like to hang on to you."

"It's good to hear. I'd like to settle down here in

Charleston if I can keep a steady flow of work."

"I'm sure we can do something about that."

Sarah Highsmith and her partner Savannah were the last to arrive. Sarah greeted all of the assemblage with, "Hi ho! We have something to celebrate – in fact, we have several somethings to celebrate, so why are you standing around looking awkward?"

Nate grinned and grabbed a bottle of champagne out of an ice bucket beside the table with hors d'oeuvres laid out on it. He popped the cork and filled eight flutes, which Georgia handed around. "To success on all fronts for Hobcaw Point!"

"Hear, hear," the other guests said, loud and clear.

The hors d'oeuvres were lovely—miniature deviled crab cakes, pickled shrimp, smoked pork belly, pickled okra and, of course, the mandatory pimento cheese spread. After killing off another bottle of champagne, the guests sat down for a proper dinner. They were served by smiling waiters in black slacks and vests, white shirts, and black ties, all wearing happy smiles as they quietly brought each course and kept the wine glasses filled. First was she crab soup, laced with sherry and served with a glass of sherry to wash it down. The next course was wahoo lightly sauteed in butter with dill and a topping of bacon, small shrimp, baby scallops, and grape tomatoes served over a bed of crab rice. An ice-cold Riesling washed it down. Next came tournedos topped with a piece of grilled warm water lobster and bearnaise sauce with a side of grilled asparagus and creamed potatoes, accompanied by an extraordinary cabernet sauvignon. Dessert was key lime pie, with a lovely, delicate Coburn's port and coffee. By the time they were done, no one could move!

As they were sitting back, chatting about simple things

and trying to digest the feast that Nate's chef had produced, David looked at Caitlin and asked, "Tell me, Cait, would you be willing to sell the county part of the land on the Wando River for the proposed yacht club? We do need the facility, just not sitting in the middle of a historical site."

"If you put it over on the Wando, it will be less expensive to build and easier to maintain too," Amanda added thoughtfully.

"I have been so focused on trying to find the deed and keeping Pinkney's hands off the family legacy that I haven't considered selling any of the plantation, but if the price was right for the part that wasn't part of the shipyard, I'd certainly consider it."

"Good, good. Let's get this whole thing about the ownership cleared up, then will you come talk with the council?"

"Of course."

SATURDAY MORNING FOUND Amanda staring at Caitlin with terror in her eyes.

"Amanda, if you're gonna stay here in Charleston, you're gonna have to be social. You can't wear business suits or khaki shorts and hiking boots to most things we go to. It just isn't done. And yes, your silvery-gray suit is lovely and you look fantastic in it, but you need more clothes."

"But, Caitlin, sweetheart, I hate shopping. I REALLY hate shopping. Can't I just give you my sizes and—"

"Amanda Sherman, get a grip, woman. Now, go put on one of your two pairs of decent slacks, a blouse that is NOT made of knitted cotton, and your loafers. We ARE going shopping."

Amanda slunk into the bedroom of her apartment, where they had come to let her change into fresh clothing for the day. She rummaged in her closet for the slacks and shoes Caitlin had ordered her to put on, then flipped through her meager collection of blouses, emerging a few minutes later in navy linen slacks, a short-sleeved light blue blouse, and black loafers with no socks.

They walked downstairs and climbed into Caitlin's car, because Caitlin said that, first, she knew where they were going, and second, Amanda's Jeep was too grubby for getting new clothes.

'But it's not too grubby to take her out on a date,' Amanda thought, smiling gently. Caitlin was in control and Amanda thought she was very cute when she was like this. As long as it didn't happen too often and she didn't turn into a younger version of her mother, this was fun.

Caitlin ran them up to Calhoun, over the Ashley River and on to the Savannah Highway, getting off at Citadel Mall, and swung around to the back to park behind Dillard's huge department store.

Caitlin marched them into the store and straight up the escalator to the second floor, which was all women's clothing as far as Amanda could see. Finding something she liked in the midst of this sea of many-colored fabric was going to be worse than finding a needle in a hay stack. At least the needle was shiny and the hay wasn't. Here, everything looked shiny.

Caitlin walked up to a woman behind one of the counters filled with perfume in the middle of the room. The clerk looked up and smiled. "Good morning, Dr. Balle. What can I do for you today?"

"Is Miss Prevost in today?"

"Yes, I believe she is. Would you like me to page her?"

"If you don't mind."

Amanda stood behind Caitlin, looking a little lost as they waited for the requested woman to appear. A few minutes later, a petite woman with curly blue-black hair, penetrating ice blue eyes, and the palest complexion Amanda had ever seen walked briskly up to the counter. She was clearly descended from one of the French families that had come to Charleston in the late 1600s. Obviously, the genes had bred true, as Miss Prevost looked like one of those portraits of French aristocratic women. She also looked vaguely familiar to Amanda.

"Ah, Dr. Balle. How good to see you again!" The effusive woman wrapped Caitlin in a delicate hug. "How can I help you today? I have some beautiful tea dresses just in for the fall season."

"I'm not here for me today, Sophira. I'd like you to meet my friend, Amanda Sherman. She needs a proper party wardrobe."

"Ah, Miss Sherman, a pleasure to see you again. I've been dressing Dr. Balle since her coming out party. How did that outfit you got when you were here with Dr. Highsmith work out for you?"

Amanda was a little embarrassed to not have recognized Miss Prevost, but that had been a rather difficult day for her.

Caitlin broke in. "Oh, Miss Prevost, did you put that outfit together? It's absolutely perfect for my friend. Can we rely on you to find three or four more equally suitable ensembles for Amanda?"

"I think we can do something for her." She turned to Amanda, surveying her rather lanky form judiciously. "With your coloring... humm. I assume you do not prefer dresses?"

"If I can avoid them, I do. But I know sometimes I won't be able to escape." Amanda chuckled.

"Not in Charleston society. I think I can fit you out so you only have to suffer wearing stockings occasionally, though. Come this way, girls." Miss Prevost led them to the back of the big room, to a small sitting area outside the fitting rooms. "If you'll have a seat, I'll have some tea brought for you while I see about finding something appropriate for you, Miss Sherman."

The little woman bustled off, rather like a lovely little bird intent on tending her young. A moment later, another woman appeared carrying a tray with a teapot and two cups and saucers on it.

"Miss Prevost. Humm. I assume from one of the old Huguenot families?" Amanda queried.

"Oh, no. Miss Prevost is Catholic. Her ancestor, for whom she is named, was the daughter of the Lt. Governor of Santo Domingo. She was smuggled out of Port-au-Prince around 1800 and put on an English trading ship to get her out of a very violent environment. The original Sophira spoke no English, and the captain spoke no French, so he put her off at the first port he called at with French speaking people. Unfortunately, it was Charleston, and there was no love for Catholics. She ended up apprenticed to a mantilla maker, had an affair with a Jewish merchant, bore him a bunch of illegitimate children, and the Prevost family was founded here in Charleston. At least one member of each generation is an exceptionally talented dresser. I think there's been a Miss Prevost at Dillard's, and before that at Ivey's, since the 1800s. A Miss Prevost dressed both of my grandmothers!"

"So she's part of your family history," laughed Amanda.

"Yup, and I expect it will continue for at least a few more generations."

"You really want to have children?"

"With the right partner, yes. How about you?"

"I expect so. I want to take some little ones out to dig in the muck."

"So, I'm the one who will have to take them to cotillion?"

"If I had my druthers, neither of us will take them to cotillion."

The two women looked at each another and started laughing, albeit rather nervously.

Very softly, and with a little bit of wonder in her voice, Amanda asked, "Are we really far enough along to be talking children?"

Before either of them could say anything else, Miss Prevost came bustling back with two younger women following behind. All three of them had their arms full of clothes.

Amanda turned her attention to Miss Prevost, who was clearly planning to clean out her checking account, wondering if she ever managed to walk without bustling. Her own grandmother could mill all by herself, so she guessed Miss Prevost was like that.

Three hours later they walked out of Dillard's carrying several clothing bags. There were three very attractive pants outfits, five blouses, two cocktail dresses, and shoes and stockings to go with them. Amanda's bank account was in mourning for its departed colleagues.

"You did real well, honey." Caitlin was looking extremely pleased. "I think Miss Prevost made some lovely selections that match your personality very well."

"She's good, I'll give her that. I think that I have myself a shopper, and given how much I love to shop, I guess that's a good thing. Just for you, I'll limit my shopping at REI to field clothes."

Caitlin laughed. "Ah, the sacrifices we make..."

Amanda looked at Caitlin out of the corner of her eye, wondering what Caitlin had almost said and if it was bitten off because she didn't feel it or if she was scared to say it. She hoped it was fear. "So, it's after one and I'm hungry. What do you say we find some lunch?"

"That's a great idea – and it's my treat since I just put a major crimp in your bank account."

"I won't argue about the crimp, but you didn't do it – I agreed to it. I want to make a life here in Charleston," she said and, in her mind, she added, 'with you.'

Caitlin retraced their steps of the morning to Calhoun Street, then turned on King Street and scooted a few blocks down to Market Street. "This is Henry's on the Market. Some say it is the best she-crab soup around – and they serve the same recipe over at Hank's Seafood."

"Well, you've converted me, you know. I've eaten more seafood and more types of seafood in the past two months than I think I have in the rest of my whole life." Amanda laughed. "And I love it."

BY MID-AFTERNOON, Pinkney and the dredging crew had found four more gold coins. They continued to dredge, sucking down until they hit the rotting hull of the old vessel, then slowly widening their pattern. They now had about a fifteen-foot-wide hole, filled with murky, muddy water, and a huge pile of junk that had been caught in the mesh of the filter. Pinkney was exhausted, soaked, covered in mud, and determined to keep going.

Raymond had changed crews that morning, sending the night crew home for some sleep. They were due back around seven. He came over to Pinkney wearing a very determined look. "Okay, Henry. There's a cot in the barge shack. Go use it or I will shut down the dredge pumps."

"You wouldn't do that. You CAN'T do that!"

"I can and I will. You are so tired you're a risk to yourself and to my crew. Go sleep. I'll watch the sieve."

It was exactly four o'clock when Pinkney went to lie down. One minute later, he was sound asleep.

The night crew came on at six o'clock and started moving up from the stern toward mid-ship. It was possible that the crew had tried to save the chest of gold when the fire broke out and then left it on the deck, or maybe it was strapped to the mast for safety.

Something woke Pinkney up around eight – a strange sound, or more accurately, a lack of sound. He came staggering out of the shack to see the whole crew gathered around the huge diesel driven pump.

The pump was not pumping.

"What the hell!" he screamed.

"We've sucked up something that clogged the pump. We'll have to clear it before we can continue."

"Well, be quick about it. Wake me when you start up again." He stomped back into the shack and the waiting cot.

Ronan grinned. 'That chunk of charred mast will take them a while to clear. I think I'll ask Tiernan to send his little masked friends over later this evening. They should find new and interesting ways to annoy the dredging crew'

Birch went to check on his weeping willow sprouts. He was pleased when they reported that they had reached the joints in the pipes that had been laid to provide water to and remove sewage from the trailer. He instructed them to open the joints, so they obediently inserted their roots and pried the seams open. Water, both clean and suffused with human excrement, began to seep up through the ground. By morning, there would be a new and rather aromatic pond at Hobcaw Point. It would make Pinkney getting his car out from behind the trailer rather difficult.

Midnight came and it was time for Ciara to exercise her vocal cords. If she didn't practice once in a while, the ability to make human beings' skin crawl would fade, and if she lost that ability, she herself would fade. Tonight was a good time to practice, she thought. She loved watching the terrified men flee from the barge.

As they fled, Pinkney cursed. Ciara laughed, a sound that was even scarier than her shrieks.

Raymond turned to Pinkney. "If we are going to clear this mess, with half the crew running off, you're gonna have to get your hands dirty. Come on, let's get back to it."

∼

AMANDA LAY IN BED, happy, sated, and looking forward to making a life for herself in this wonderful old city. Caitlin lay cuddled against her, head on her shoulder, issuing forth with tiny little snores that almost sounded like a cat's purr. Life was good.

BY THREE IN THE MORNING, the skeleton crew finally managed to pull the shredded chunks of oak out of the suction tube. They carefully lowered the hose back into the murky water, then Pinkney ran back to his position beside the sieve to wash away the mud and try to find more gold. For the next four hours, they made slow progress. Pinkney found a lot of charred wood and various miscellaneous pieces of ships fittings, but no more gold.

Ronan smirked.

As the sun came up, the day crew started to return, cursing a blue streak about the new pond that had formed where the parking area had once been. Pinkney look alarmed, worried about his car. While the crew handed off for the day, he jogged up to the trailer. His car was completely blocked in by the new pond.

Birch giggled.

CAITLIN WOKE up as the sun invaded her room. She smiled, loving the feeling of waking up in Amanda's arms. Yes, it had only been a couple of months, but this was so comfortable and comforting. There was something special about Amanda. They had fit together so easily from the beginning. They worked together well, they played together well, they socialized together well, and damn, the sex was fantastic. There was something in their love making that was different from anyone else she'd ever been with, not that there were that many samples. The emotional connection with Amanda was amazing.

Caitlin looked at the woman lying with her arms loosely wrapped around her. 'Am I actually falling in love? Could this work for the long run? God, I think so. I hope so.'

Later that morning they headed out to Sullivan's Island for brunch at a rather unique restaurant named The Obstinate Daughter after an English cartoon from 1776 that depicted "Miss Carolina Sulivan, one of the obstinate daughters of America," with cannon embedded in her massive hair-do. The place was famous for its brunch menu, and Sullivan's Island was beautiful.

Caitlin had a piece of quiche and Amanda a bowl of Frogmore chowder. For dessert, they split one of the O/D's famous sweet rolls.

They finished eating at about half past eleven, and decided to go for a walk on the beach. The sun was bright, and as so often happened in South Carolina, the September day was hot, but a fresh breeze was blowing in off the ocean, and both women were dressed for the weather. Bare feet playing in the edge of the surf provided additional cooling.

They had driven down to the lighthouse to avoid the crowds at the public beach. There were only a few people on this beach, and they walked toward Fort Moultrie Park, past the nature trail and the trees and bushes that lined the shore. As the number of people continued to thin out, Caitlin hesitantly slipped her hand into Amanda's, reveling in the warmth and comfort that that hand gave her.

"You've been awful quiet. Is something bothering you?" Amanda was a little concerned about how quiet her usually talkative friend had been as they walked. The hand in hers helped, but she was still a little nervous.

"I've been thinking. You're gonna be here for the long term, aren't you?"

"I'd like to be. It looks like I can work here for pretty much as long as I want, with help from Spencer and David and Nate."

"I'd like you to be," Caitlin said softly. She took a deep breath and jumped off what she saw as a cliff. "You probably need something better than that little apartment, you know, a better place to live. Would you like to, um, move in with me when your lease is up?"

Amanda stopped cold, stunned. Happy, but stunned. "You want me to live with you?"

Caitlin shrugged. "Well, we get along really well." She took another deep breath. "I really like waking up with you," she said in a small voice. In an even smaller voice, she added, "And you survived my mother pretty well."

Amanda blinked – several times. It was close, but not everything she wanted. She wanted everything, and knew it. "Honey, you have been so brave, standing up to your mother. Are you ready to keep doing it? Because if I move in, she'll go ballistic."

"I don't care if she goes ballistic. I lo..like being with you."

Amanda reached out and took both of Caitlin's hands in hers. "Sweetie, I'm a kind of strange duck. I've never committed to anyone, never lived with anyone – even in college, I had my own room in the dorm. I've never shared, because I know if I do – no, when I do, it will be permanent – for life. As much as I want that with you – and I truly do want that with you, are you ready for forever?"

Caitlin looked down at their joined hands and let her mind float over all the things they had together, about Amanda standing up for her, laughing with her, loving her with a passion she'd never experienced before, about her tenderness and the strength beneath her gentle presence. And now, about what she heard Amanda offering – forever.

She looked into those warm brown eyes that shone with a tender acceptance that she knew she needed more than anything else in her life. "I love you, Amanda. I'm in love with you."

Amanda smiled softly. "I know, sweetheart. I trust your love, but are you ready for commitment? Because I'm already here for the long term."

Caitlin looked deeper into Amanda's eyes. "Are you saying you love me? That you want to be with me for good?"

"I'm saying exactly that. I love you. If I move in, I'm never moving out unless you pitch me out."

They had much more to say to each another, much more to learn, but for now, it was enough and more than enough to just hold one another.

RONAN WAS FEELING A LITTLE UNCOMFORTABLE. As much as he kept throwing obstacles in their way, the dredgers were getting too close to the gold for his comfort. If they kept at it for another night, they might actually find it. He slipped over to the cemetery and hailed Siobhan.

"Madam, it is time for you to send the ladies over to catch the miscreants."

"Are they getting that close?"

"Aye, I fear so. We have harassed them, but they persist."

"Then I shall do what I can."

Siobhan searched for the energy signatures of Amanda and Caitlin, and popped herself off to where they were. She grinned and clapped her hands soundlessly as she saw them entwined at the edge of the ocean. Clearly, they had moved to a new place in their growing relationship, but now she needed to nudge them in a different direction.

"OUCH!" Caitlin hopped back from the water's edge and brushed the fiddler crab that had attached itself to her little toe.

A moment later, Amanda did the same dance with the little crustaceans. She laughed as she brushed one off her heel. "I think they're trying to give us a message. Time to head back?"

"I guess so."

Laughing, they jogged back up the beach till they reached the boardwalk that would take them back to the car – and their shoes.

"Hey, since we're over in this direction, why don't we go look at the part of the plantation on the Wando – get an idea of what David wants the county to buy?"

"I'd be glad to show it to you. I've been working on what could be done over there for the commissioners and can explain what I think they should do."

"Great, let's go."

Amanda drove into the Point, but from a different direction than she usually went, taking a more direct route to the Wando River side of the property.

Hobcaw Drive was almost a circle, curving around to bring them up to the Wando River side of the Point, before it swung back to the site of the old shipyard. Amanda stopped closest to the actual river. "Come on and let me show you."

They parked under a tree on the side of the road and Amanda led the way over toward the river. "I thought the club house could go here, with the closest access to the street, so that things like power and water and sewage would be the easiest to lay, and it would be easier to get to for social events. If we put the pool behind it, they'd have a nice view over the pool and out to the river. The parking and storage for smaller boats could go there, with a boat ramp between a couple of docks into the mouth of the creek for larger boats but protected in bad weather. And this way, none of it touches the area that was the old shipyard."

As Amanda talked, they walked toward the mouth of Hobcaw Creek where it opened onto the Wando.

Caitlin frowned. "What's that noise?"

Amanda stopped and listened. "If I didn't know better, it sounds like the dredgers, but they weren't supposed to be working this weekend."

They slipped back to the tree line and worked their way down the creek till they could see the old harbor without being seen by anyone who might be there.

"Son of a bitch!" Amanda's curse was vehement even if it was said quietly.

"What is that?" Caitlin was confused.

"That, my love, is the dredging crew, dredging on your property without permission, and I can see Mr. Henry Pinkney at the sorting screen."

"I've had enough of that little slimeball. Don't go break it up – let's just call the cops."

"Okay."

Within ten minutes, Amanda and Caitlin met the uniformed patrol car at the entrance to the normal parking area for the trailer. It was impassable. Within a couple of minutes, David Gibbs and Spencer Rowe pulled up behind them.

The officers looked at the pond Birch's little sprouts had created and scratched their heads. "I can hear the dredge, ma'am, but how do we get around this pond of sewage?"

At David's request, Caitlin waited for three more people to join them. When Caitlin called them and told him what they'd seen, he had contacted several other members of the county council and asked them to join him. When they arrived, the whole troop of people was ready to go and confront the illegal dredgers – and eager to find out what the hell Pinkney was doing.

"Follow me, gentlemen." Amanda gestured for them to follow her and they tromped around the oversized puddle.

Amanda led her little group single file along a narrow animal trail that took them around the back side of the trailer and toward the mud flat where the dry dock had once been. They all saw Pinkney's rather distinctive Caddy, parked in sewage halfway up its hubcaps. Several snorts of amused derision could be heard.

Amanda swung back toward the old harbor and within a few minutes, the entire group could see the dredging crew pulling up tons of muck and evidently being very excited. Pinkney' was very obviously sorting through the refuse being sucked up. His eagerness was apparent as he plucked objects out of the muck in the sieve as fast as he could and tossed them in a large plastic bucket beside him.

The folks with Amanda and Caitlin looked at one another with surprised and somewhat bewildered looks.

David took the lead. "Whatever he's sucking up there, it's Dr. Balle's property, the dredging is not authorized, and at minimum, they're trespassing and may be stealing historically valuable artifacts. Do your duty, gentlemen."

The two cops looked at one another and grinned. Pinkney wasn't the only person on the barge they recognized. "Cease and desist your operations. Everybody, put your hands up. You are under arrest for trespassing."

CHAPTER 12

THE POLICE IMMEDIATELY CALLED FOR BACKUP. They were arresting a crew of six men plus one of the county's commissioners for trespassing and attempted theft. They knew better than to try to handle this mess by themselves, especially with most of the county commission standing behind them watching.

Within a matter of minutes, two more squad cars and the chief of police pulled up. Amanda obligingly went and guided them around the sewage pond. As they walked around the mess, the chief called the county works team to get out a crew to deal with the sewage.

Once the entire team of law enforcement officials assembled, the chief instructed Raymond to come over in the jon boat. One of her boys would then ferry the rest of the miscreants over a couple at a time.

"Um, Chief?" David Gibbs tapped him on his shoulder. "I'd like to see what they were dredging up. I know it's Dr. Balle's property, but this is going to be a complicated mess and I'd like to know just what Pinkney's been after all this time."

"Sure, Dave. Ride over after Terry's got the dredge crew out, when he goes to get Pinkney."

Police Chief Graham Gaillard had a slightly warped sense of humor and roundly detested Henry Pinkney. Making the annoying man sweat was entirely amusing to her.

"Thanks, Gray. Wait till you hear the whole story on this one. It'll be fascinating. And have one of your fraud boys on hand. I think our dear prosecutor Marie de Saussure will be amazed."

"You don't say. Well, I look forward to that." Gray Gaillard turned her attention to her troops, who were reading their rights to the dredging crew and lining them up on solid ground before they got marched out to jail.

Terry Gabeau poled the little boat over to the barge with David Gibbs. Both of them looked forward to taking the sweating slimeball into custody, though for different reasons. They stepped on the barge and casually strolled over to the bucket that Pinkney had been so eagerly filling.

Gold coins, and by the look of things, lots of them.

David tossed through the detritus in the sieve and found several more coins, which he added to the bucket. He looked at one of the coins and realized that what he had in his hand was from the Civil War era and before.

He looked at Pinkney, who was now handcuffed and ready to be put on the jon boat. "I thought you were after contracting kick-backs; I was wrong. This is Confederate gold. THIS is what you've been after all the time! The whole yacht club thing was just an excuse to get your hands on this property and the gold."

Pinkney just glared at Gibbs and kept his mouth shut. Monk would have to bail him out.

David looked at the other county commissioners, who had been watching the activities of the past hour with fascination. His expression was questioning, and as he looked at each commissioner in turn, they nodded. "Caitlin Balle, Charleston County is dropping the eminent domain action against the property known as Hobcaw Point. You have provided clear evidence that your family has owned this property continuously since 1684, and that all taxes have been duly paid. Though the property is currently deemed unimproved, the family cemetery has been maintained. Further, the property has been placed on the National Register of Historic Places and is of no potential benefit to the county."

Gray Gaillard bent over and picked up a handful of the gold coins. "I'd say you're a pretty wealthy woman, Cait. What a fortuitous outcome of that slime's activities." She grinned at her family friend. "Your mother will be absolutely green with envy."

The officers loaded Pinkney into one of the squad cars. He was cursing all the way, muttering, "You can't do this to me. I'm a county commissioner, for God's sake."

Gaillard turned to Amanda and Caitlin. "Ladies, I know this has been a trying day for the two of you. I would appreciate it if you would come over to the station tomorrow, when I can have one of the representatives from the prosecutor's office there, to give us your statements."

Spencer laughed. "Marie may want to be there herself.

She's never been overly fond of Pinkney either." He turned to Caitlin and Amanda. "I'll go with you." It was not an offer; it was an order that Caitlin knew would have to be obeyed. He turned back to the chief. "I expect you to remember that that gold is Dr. Balle's and mark it as such in evidence. Do I need to send someone over to help you count it?"

Gray grinned at Spencer as she shook her head. She knew how carefully the attorney took care of his clients, but this was a crime scene, and the odds were good that there was more gold under the mud given the rate that it was being pumped out of the flats. "I'll be putting a guard on the site. If there's any more gold down there, it's evidence in a criminal case, and I'd prefer it if none of the local mud daubers came out to try and collect until we can bring it up properly. I assure you, Cait's gold is safe."

"Good. I'll get in touch with Sarah Highsmith. She can guide us about proper handling of what is obviously a historic site. That is, if that meets with your approval, Caitlin." David was going by the book on this one. Even though they were friends, Caitlin probably had grounds for a very nasty suit against the county because of Pinkney's actions.

The cluster of people down by the harbor heard the sound of heavy machinery and the tell-tale clanking of a backhoe. "Oh, good. The waterworks boys are here. That sewage leak needs to be fixed soon, before it pollutes the creek even worse that it is, from all the digging and raw pumping Pinkney's crew did." Gray looked pleased.

She looked around at her staff. "Okay – you two get to stand watch. I'll see about sending you out some drinks and sandwiches and have you relieved in a few hours. Don't let anyone on that barge unless I come with them personally."

The men nodded, murmuring, "Yes, Chief. We'll watch it."

"I suspect there's someone else involved in this little soap opera, and I'd like to find out who the easy way."

"Yes, ma'am. We'll watch – discretely."

"Good man."

AMANDA AND CAITLIN walked back up to Hobcaw Drive, where they'd moved the car when they were waiting for the police. "What do you say we go home, get rid of the sweat, salt, sand, and mud, and then go get some dinner? A nice, small, romantic restaurant would be a good idea, I think."

"Yeah, Pinkney kinda spoiled the mood, didn't he?" Caitlin smiled a little wistfully.

Amanda stopped them both, and regardless of who might see them, took Caitlin in her arms. "Caitlin, my love, you told me you love me and want a life with me. They could have dropped an atomic bomb and I'd still be flying higher than a kite." She smiled and tenderly kissed Caitlin.

"Wow! You sure know how to shift a mood, you romantic thing, you." Caitlin stroked Amanda's cheek, then ran her fingers through her sandy colored hair. "Home, shower, and a romantic dinner sounds perfect."

They were home within less than a half hour. As they walked into the house, the phone was ringing. Caitlin sighed. Amanda motioned toward it, indicating that she should answer it.

"Hello."

"Caitlin! What the hell happened today? David called, said that the county was going to need my help at Hobcaw!" Sarah was almost yelling, she was so excited and confused.

Cait's laughter did nothing but irritate the archeologist.

"Come on, tell me."

"Okay, the Reader's Digest version is some Confederate gold was found, Pinkney was caught trying to steal it, the eminent domain action has been dropped, Amanda's going to build a yacht club over on the Wando, and the country's probably going to need a new architect." She said it in one breath, requiring a deep gasp to reload her lungs with oxygen. "I will tell you the whole story in the morning when I come in for work."

"I take it you have company, so I'll let you go, but you better be in early to fill me in on everything!"

"I don't have company. It's just me and Amanda here."

"Oh, ho, woman. You need to fill me in on that in the morning too. If Amanda isn't company, what is she?"

Caitlin blushed, deeply.

Amanda looked at her with a quizzical expression before awareness dawned. She took the phone from Caitlin's hand. "Hi, Sarah. You can expect me to be around for a quite a while – and around Caitlin. Can I come by tomorrow morning?"

Slightly flustered, but grinning, Sarah said, "Of course. I figure you'll be able to tell me what I'm gonna need to do for the county."

"I can – at least some of it. See you tomorrow. Bye."

Before Sarah could say anything in response, Amanda hung up the phone. "We'll deal with her tomorrow. Tonight is for us."

"I love you."

"I love you too. Now, shower."

They strolled upstairs, took a leisurely shower paying more attention to delivering caresses than actually cleaning their bodies, and got dressed. Brunch had been a long time ago.

"What say we wander over to the oyster bar, scarf down some oceanic snot, and follow it with a big bowl of bog?"

Caitlin grinned. She had converted Amanda to low-country cuisine. "Sounds perfect. Close, reasonable, private booths and good food."

"Let's go!"

"JOE, you've got to come bail me out. I found it, for the love of God, and not only is that bitch going to get it, she's going to send me to jail!"

"Henry, as far as anyone knows, I don't know you from Adam. Don't call me again." Joseph Monk hung up – decisively.

Henry Pinkney wondered if the man had broken his phone when he did.

Sighing, he quickly called his wife's cell phone.

"Hello," said a deep man's voice.

Henry was startled. Why was a man answering Sherry's cell phone? "Is Sherry there?"

"Let me see if she's available. Can I tell her who is calling?"

The man's accent was distinctly Bostonian. "Tell her it's her HUSBAND. And who the hell are you?" He was not happy.

"Hi, Henry. What do you need?"

"I need you to get my lawyer and have him meet me at the jail. I need you to come and bail me out, and I need to know who the hell you're with."

"I'll call your attorney. He can get you out of jail, and Jeffery is the man I'm leaving you for. Ta ta, Henry."

Pinkney put his head in his hands. How the hell had his life fallen apart so completely so quickly? Well, at least he'd take that damned Joe Monk with him.

CAITLIN AND AMANDA strolled home after having stuffed themselves with oysters, bog, and pimento cheese. Very gently, Amanda took Caitlin's hand in hers. "Have I told you recently that I love you? That I want to stay here in Charleston because of you? That I want to run out to a jewelry store and buy you a ring? That today may have been busy and complicated and strange, but it has been the best day of my life? Do you really want me to live with you? Forever?"

Caitlin smiled gently at the woman who sounded so hopeful and happy at her side. "I do. I truly do. Forever sounds pretty good to me."

Amanda stopped in the middle of the sidewalk, took Caitlin in her arms, picked her up, and spun her around.

Laughing, Caitlin commanded, "Put me down, you goose. And yes, live with me. I love you. Stop being so insecure – you got the girl!"

~

ON MONDAY MORNING, Spencer was in Judge Monk's court, holding the validated deed in one hand, and with David beside him to withdraw the eminent domain suit on behalf of Charleston County.

"Your honor, we have validated the deed to Hobcaw Plantation, including the boundary definitions as being a valid document from 1684 and signed by three of the original landgraves of the Colony of South Carolina. It has been validated by the historical laboratories of Harvard University." He produced the documentation from Harvard. "This deed has held for the entire time from then until now, and we have presented proof that the family has paid all applicable taxes since 1868, which is as far back as the tax records can be traced, because the records before then were burned at the end of the Civil War in 1865."

Monk looked at the papers that Spencer and David had first passed to his clerk, who then handed them to him. "Mr. Rowe, these all seem to be in order. This court acknowledges the ownership of the property called Hobcaw Plantation, stretching from the shore of the Wando River to the beginning of the delta of Hobcaw Creek, including all facilities, resources, and minerals, natural or man-made." Judge Joseph Monk had to struggle to get that statement out without gritting his teeth. Caitlin Balle had the gold, free and clear. This after his family had waited for five generations to collect on their carefully guarded secret.

David Gibbs stepped up then. "Your honor, in light of this information, Charleston County withdraws its claims of eminent domain for this property and acknowledges the legal ownership of the property belongs to Dr. Caitlin Balle."

"This court acknowledges Charleston County's withdrawal of the eminent domain claim on the property called Hobcaw Point." Monk hesitated, then had to ask, "So, what about the plan for a yacht club?"

David Gibbs grinned. There was the clue he was looking for. "Since the original site has been listed on the National Register of Historic Properties, we could not build a yacht club there regardless of property ownership. At the recommendation of our civil engineer, we will be looking to acquire the portion of the property that faces the Wando River and is not part of the historic site. Actually, it will be more economical and provide users easier access. All told, it is a better solution for the county."

"So, the county gets its yacht club and Dr. Balle keeps the historic part of the site?"

"Yes, your honor."

"Well, I wish you luck, sir. This session is adjourned and all actions are withdrawn. Good day, gentlemen." He turned to his clerk. "Mr. Harmond, will you attend to the paperwork, please?"

Monk retreated to his office, pulled off his robes, and dropped into his chair. He put his head in his hands, gritting his teeth. That idiot Pinkney had ruined everything. Now he wondered if this idiot's screw ups would get him disbarred.

AT THREE O'CLOCK, Caitlin and Spencer walked into the police station with Amanda trailing behind. Marie de Saussure, the county prosecutor, had freed up her schedule to sit in on the interviews that afternoon.

Ms. de Saussure had gone through all the paperwork that had been filed with the court. To her, the fact that the county's own civil engineer had stated that the old shipyard site was not optimal for a new recreational yacht club and the fact that the plan Pinkney had put forward would destroy any historical significance of the site were both indicative of an ulterior motive.

Amanda's testimony on the interference from Pinkney and his efforts to implement more changes than were legal prior to completion of the eminent domain claim were duly noted by Ms. de Saussure.

They then got to the events of Sunday afternoon. Pinkney's presence on the barge, and the fact that it was not the usual barge crew were all indicative of illicit activity. Police Chief Gaillard had been doing some serious poking into Pinkney's activities. One fascinating piece of information was Pinkney's phone records. They included multiple calls to and from Judge Joseph Monk's private number – the same Joseph Monk who was presiding over the eminent domain case.

Ms. De Saussure looked at her notes and shook her head. "You should know that we have looked at Judge Monk's role in this mess very carefully. Mr. Pinkney had a great deal to say about how Judge Monk betrayed him, and how all of this was Monk's idea, but all we can prove is that Monk's family knew about the gold from the day the ship sank. One of his ancestor's was the ship's cabin boy, and the story was passed down from father to son in his family. He told Pinkney about the gold and he maneuvered to have the eminent domain case assigned to his docket, but the fact of the matter is that he never actually did anything outright illegal. He did not file the suit, he did nothing to convince the county board to take on the project, he did not plan the dredging operation – all of that was Pinkney. Monk simply provided Pinkney with the information about the location of the gold. The only thing he did that was technically a violation of his position as an officer of the court was to have a case assigned to him when he had a personal interest in it. Even then, he did nothing illegal. In fact, he ruled in favor of Mr. Rowe's motions in this case. So, the only thing we can do is to bring him before the Bar. He loses his seat as a judge and he loses his right to practice law in South Carolina. Otherwise..." She shrugged. "He is a very smart crook."

Just then, Gray hauled in the bucket of coins, straining at the weight. "I had Sarah Highsmith come over and look at these this morning. I also had a numismatist come over and appraise them. We counted over 850 coins and we think there are more down there. At today's prices in just pure gold, that bucket is worth about nine hundred thousand dollars. However, since these coins are in excellent condition since they've been protected by the mud, each one is worth between, say, thirty thousand and over a hundred thousand, with an average estimated by the coin dealer around sixty thousand each. You may be looking at about fifty million, dear. And it's all yours."

Caitlin, who had stood up to look in the bucket, sat

back down very abruptly. Fifty million was a whole lot of money.

Amanda reached out and gently touched Caitlin's shoulder. "Caitlin? Are you okay?"

Caitlin looked at her, blinking rather like an owl and muttered, "Fifty? Million?"

Gray said, "When we get it all up out of the mud, probably more."

Caitlin was still trying and failing to process the information. "Fifty?"

Amanda looked at the people in the room. "I think I better just get her home and let this soak in. I assume the gold has to stay with you as evidence for a while."

Gray smiled. "Yes, it does, but we will be keeping it in a vault and we carry insurance to cover all appraised evidence." She handed Amanda a small pile of papers. "She needs to hang on to these. Take her home, get her to relax. Personally, I'd recommend a shot or three of good bourbon."

Spencer rose to give Amanda a hand with the dumbfounded Caitlin. "I'll file those papers eventually, but for now, why don't you keep them so you can convince Miss Dumbstruck here that it's real?"

"Good idea, Spencer. Let us know when the official papers come back about the court case being dismissed too. She's going to have to figure out what to do, especially given David's offer to buy part of the land for the county."

AMANDA PULLED INTO THE DRIVEWAY, where she found a familiar looking silver BMW sedan parked in her usual spot. She parked so as not to block the ever-annoying Mrs. Balle's car.

Caitlin was still just staring into space. Amanda gently shook her shoulder. "Caitlin, you need to rejoin the living. Your mother is here."

"Oh, my God. Fifty million and my mother in one day?"

"I'm right here. Shall we go face the, um, music?"

Amanda got out of the car and went around to hand Caitlin out. She thought, wryly, that it was a good thing she'd worn one of the nice outfits that Miss Prevost had chosen for her to meet with the county prosecutor. It was entirely appropriate for confronting Mrs. Balle.

They went into the kitchen and Caitlin called out, "Mother?"

"I'm in the library, dear." Mrs. Balle was sounding perfectly ordinary.

"Do you want some limeade?"

"That sounds lovely."

Caitlin looked at Amanda. Her eyes spoke volumes, and in particular, asked, 'Who is this person and what happened to my mother?'

Amanda got a tray while Caitlin pulled glasses from the cabinet. Ice followed, and she poured three glasses of limeade, which Amanda put on the tray. She picked it up and nodded toward the door.

They walked into the library. A brief look of discomfort flashed on Mrs. Balle's face, but was replaced with a pleasant smile, one that failed to reach her eyes, though. Amanda sat the tray down on the coffee table in front of Mrs. Balle, then sat down beside Caitlin on the sofa.

"So, Mother, what brings you here today?" Caitlin was definitely suspicious and it showed in her tone of voice.

"Well, I was at the club for lunch today and I heard all sorts of stories about excitement out at Hobcaw and wanted to make sure you were all right."

"Yes, we had an interesting time yesterday," Caitlin replied cautiously. "Fortunately, no one was hurt and we're both fine today."

Harriet looked at Amanda and rather stiffly said, "It's a pleasure to see you again, Miss Sherman."

"Good afternoon, Mrs. Balle. I trust you are doing well."

One could have cut the forced politeness in the room with a knife.

"I heard that Henry Pinkney has been arrested for trespassing and other charges. Is that true?"

"Yes. Amanda and I have just come from a meeting with Marie de Saussure about it. Because there's a legal case involved, I'm afraid we can't discuss it, though."

"Not even with your mother? That's appalling! A mother should be allowed to know everything." Harriet sounded offended that her daughter could not tell her all the good dirt.

"I'm sorry, but no, I can't discuss it."

Harriet turned to Amanda. "So, Miss Sherman, does all of this mean your position with the county is over? I mean, with the site being on the register, and Pinkney's position so precarious..."

"Thank you for your concern, Mrs. Balle, but my contract with the county is for three years and is not project-specific. However, I will be overseeing the new yacht club, just not on the site of the old shipyard. I believe the county will be making an offer for the land over on the Wando, so I will be around for a while."

"Oh. How convenient for you," Harriet responded with absolutely no enthusiasm.

Caitlin got an evil grin on her face. "Yes, you will be seeing a lot more of Amanda in the future. She has agreed to move in with me here."

"Oh," Harriet said numbly. "You decided you needed a roommate?"

"No, Mother." She paused for effect. "I decided I need a mate."

The silence in the room was stunning.

"A mate?" Harriet finally asked in a confused voice.

"Yes. A mate. A partner. A companion. A spouse. A wife. A mate." Caitlin smiled sweetly at Amanda. "Amanda suits me very well. She's loving, and gentle, and incredibly intelligent, and sweet, and kind, and I love her."

"But, Caitlin," Harriet wailed. "You can't marry a woman."

"Companions have been part of Charleston society for years. You know as well as I do it is a perfectly acceptable social relationship."

"But, Caitlin – not only is she a woman, she's not our kind of people! SHE'S A SHERMAN!" Harriet wept. "How could you do this to me, to us? We'll be pariahs in society."

"I doubt that, Mother. Amanda has been very well received by the folks in town."

"You mean you've been introducing her to our friends?"

"Yes, I have."

"I've become good friends with some of them – Sarah Highsmith, David Gibbs, Nate and Georgia Wyche, Daniel

Amy, Helen Sothel, and other members of the historical commission. As a matter of fact, I believe I'll be working with Sarah's partner Savannah, as she is currently the leading candidate to architect the new yacht club." Amanda smiled sweetly. She was perfectly aware that name dropping was the favorite lubricant for Harriet's soul.

"Well, I don't have to be a party to this... this... this social disaster of yours. Anyway, all she wants is your money. She'll be gone as soon as she's drained you dry."

"Oh, yes, the money. I assume you want part of the money, Mother. I know Amanda isn't after it – so, you'll accept us if you want any of the gold that I know you've heard about."

Stephen Balle had left his wife comfortably well-off – a condo on Sullivan's Island and a very nice investment account, but the idea of Confederate gold was more than the socially driven woman could resist.

"That's blackmail," Harriet hissed.

"Yes, yes, it is. It is no worse than some of the things you have done to me. Remember Suzanne? What about Leslie? And what you did to Fancher made this little piece of coercion look absolutely innocent." Caitlin glared at her mother. "I am certain that it galls your soul that you will have to depend on my generosity. Let me remind you that you have no claim to anything at Hobcaw, so you have no legitimate claim to the gold."

Amanda watched the confrontation between mother and daughter as it escalated to an uncomfortable pitch. She dropped her hand on Caitlin's shoulder and quietly said, "Honey, it has been a very difficult day, and this is getting out of hand. We don't need your mother resenting you nor do you need to threaten her. She will either accept us or she won't, but buying her acceptance isn't the way to go."

Amanda turned to Harriet. "Mrs. Balle, please understand. I love your daughter very much and I made my commitment to her before we had any idea about the gold. I have done my best to protect the Balle legacy at Hobcaw, and I have done my best to protect Caitlin from Henry Pinkney. If she lets me, I will do my best to care for her and protect her for the rest of our lives. If you can accept that, then I'm sure you will be welcome in our home. I hope you will be a good grandmother to our children. But if you can't accept us, I understand that too, and I will do my best to ease the pain you will cause Caitlin if you make that choice."

Harriet Balle looked at the woman sitting beside her daughter, seeing determination in her eyes. As much as she hated to admit it, Caitlin had found herself a staunch defender. As for the rest, well, time would tell.

"You two have had a difficult couple of days, and you both look tired. We will talk again later. Good evening," Harriet said as she rose with as much dignity as she could summon after Caitlin's vitriolic outburst, and quietly left the house.

"Well, that went well," Caitlin commented, with her anger at her mother still dripping from her voice.

"Your mother is the product of her time and culture. For her, social standing is everything. It does no good to get angry. Frankly, I feel sorrier for her than angry at her."

Caitlin turned to Amanda. She laid her head on that willing and welcoming shoulder. "God, how did I get so lucky? You'd forgive her almost anything, wouldn't you?"

"Caitlin, darling, please don't confuse understanding

with forgiveness. She has hurt you in all sorts of ways and I cannot forgive her for that. The worst is that she's just not a good mother – she doesn't give you the support and acceptance and unconditional love that all children deserve. But it doesn't do any good for me to get angry at her; it won't change anything and will just make the relationship you have with her even more strained. You are who is important to me. She is simply not important enough for me to waste energy on being mad at her."

Caitlin wrapped her arms around Amanda more tightly. "I love you. Come on, feed me, then let's go to bed."

EPILOGUE

"IT HAS TAKEN ALMOST THREE YEARS TO CREATE this outstanding recreational facility, a facility that Mount Pleasant and Charleston County has needed for a long time. It gives me great pleasure to officially open the Samuel Balle Club House and the Hobcaw Yacht Club. We have asked Dr. Caitlin Balle, the direct descendant of Samuel Balle, and Amanda Sherman, the engineer who managed to build this beautiful facility for our city, to cut the ribbon and declare this wonderful resource open to the public." David Gibbs, now chairman of the county council grinned and stepped aside for the two women.

Caitlin and Amanda held the oversized scissors to cut the ribbon together, then stepped over to Sarah Highsmith and Savannah Hassard to retrieve their child, little Siobhan Sherman-Balle.

"So, how is the dig going, Sarah? With all the last-minute things needed for start-up here, I've been a little busy," smiled Amanda.

"Like you haven't kept Savannah busy too. The dig is going well. It's amazing what's under that top layer of dirt! I think we'll have enough data to inform a really accurate reconstruction of a revolutionary era shipyard, just like you want, Caitlin."

"Well, you know, we certainly have profited from Pinkney being a crook," laughed Caitlin. "There's more than enough money to pay for the entire reconstruction, and we'll have a really great historical site for the public to learn something fascinating. I got a bid the other day to construct a typical merchant ship to top it off!"

"It's good that Pinkney won't be able to visit for a few more years. By the time he gets out, the whole reconstruction should be up and running. He should be able to see what his efforts made possible."

"Ah, Savannah, you are one evil woman!" Caitlin grinned at her friend.

"Oh, CAITLIN," a voice called from somewhere within the crowd.

Caitlin looked around, as did Amanda, trying to find the source of the voice.

The crowd shifted a bit and Harriet emerged. She nodded politely to all four women, then grinned at the small sandy haired child in Amanda's arms. "Here's my little pumpkin. Come to Granma, little one."

The child threw herself into her grandmother's arms, laughing as she did so. Granma spoiled her absolutely rotten. At nine months old, Siobhan knew where goodies came from. Harriet came through again, pulling a baby biscuit from a plastic bag in her purse. "Mother, you'll spoil her lunch," Caitlin rebuked her mother.

"It's my job, Caitlin. I may have been a lousy mother, but I know how to be a good grandmother."

Caitlin and Amanda both laughed, even while they gave Harriet a rather exasperated glare.

Samuel and Siobhan looked on, smiling. They quietly returned to their stones, satisfied with the outcome of this generation's efforts. The Balle legacy would go on.

HISTORICAL NOTES

Hobcaw Point is a real place. When I first saw it, it was empty marshland as I have described it in this book – complete with old oak tree, family cemetery, and supposedly a banshee. It was a shipyard as of the early 1700s and was burned down at the end of the Civil War. The Balle family heritage is based on my own family history, which dates back to the late 1600s, when at least two of my direct ancestors were landgraves who were granted land south of Virginia in 1663 under charter from King Charles II.

By 1671, the first permanent settlement, Charles Towne, had 340 men and women living at the confluence of the Ashley and Cooper Rivers. By 1685, rice was beginning to be cultivated, and by 1699, Carolina planters sent over 300 tons of rice to England. The rice crops made Charleston into a major mercantile port, and the need for a shipyard became obvious. Hobcaw Point was doing a brisk business in ship maintenance, repair and building within twenty years.

The colony was split into North and South Carolina in

1712, with South Carolina's commercial crop being rice and starting to include cotton, and North Carolina growing tobacco, which shipped through Virginia.

After years of serving the shipping community, the shipyard at Hobcaw Point contributed to the Civil War by building and maintaining small, swift blockade runners that frustrated the Union Navy all during the war.

For many years, Hobcaw was left alone, other than to maintain the family cemetery. However, as it happens with anything, modern society has slowly inserted itself. The Hobcaw Yacht Club exists – at the junction of Hobcaw Creek and the Wando River. There are several upscale homes facing the creek. It is, however, still mostly creek and marsh grass.

Let me acknowledge the shops and restaurants mentioned in this story – they are all real, and all excellent. The story of Miss Prevost is also real, and the tale of the first Miss Prevost and her relationship with Mr. Samuel Jewel, Charleston merchant, was quite the scandal in its day. (I do like my more scandalous ancestors.)

Taylor Rickard, June 2022

ALSO BY TAYLOR RICKARD

NON-FICTION

Redmond Family Cookbook (2023)

FICTION

Taylor Rickard and T. Novan

The Redmond Family Romance Series

Book 1: Words Heard in Silence

Book 2: Paths of Peace

Book 3: Enemies in the Gates

Book 4: Honor Thy Father

Book 5: Love Beareth All Things

Book 6: Whither Thou Goest

ABOUT TAYLOR RICKARD

WWW.TAYLORRICKARD.COM

Taylor Rickard has an unusual background. She was raised in the south by a grandmother whose love of Southern history and traditions was instilled in her from an early age. Her grandmother's dreams for her life included being presented at the St. Cecilia's Cotillion, marriage to a nice boy from the Citadel, and a life of doing research for the Huguenot Society of South Carolina and raising lovely little Children of the Confederacy. That didn't happen. She grew up to have multiple careers in her life.

She has been a chef, a television producer/director and an information technology architect. But it was that love and knowledge of all things southern that lead her and her partner, T. Novan to begin what would become a saga that follows the lives of a family through the end of the Civil War, the pain of the Reconstruction, and the extravagance of the Gilded Age – so far!

She now lives with her partner on a small farm in rural Kentucky, raising their oldest grandson, working her day job, writing at night, and feeding her family and friends from her extraordinary collection of traditional recipes from around the world.

www.ausxippublishing.com

AUSXIP Publishing publishes quality fiction and non-fiction with strong female characters that inspire, strengthen and enrich the soul. Stories that build up, create a sense of achievement and most importantly to entertain.

AUSXIP Publishing Newsletter
https://newsletter.ausxippublishing.com

Facebook:
https://facebook.com/ausxippublishing

Twitter:
https://twitter.com/ausxippublish